FALLING FOR THE LOST DUTCHMAN

--.--

JOSLYN CHASE

PARAQUEL PRESS

WHAT READERS ARE SAYING

ABOUT JOSLYN CHASE

"Author Joslyn Chase has now confirmed my first impressions of her being a formidable suspense writer bound to make readers sit up and take notice."

~ Manie Kilian (reader, Amazon.com)

"As always in her writing, the settings and action scenes are vividly portrayed and the relationships between the characters are seamless and authentic. Ms Chase has a talent for bringing characters to life."

~ ReadnGrow

"There is a reason Chase is an award-winning author. Highly recommended."

~ Justin Boote, author of *Badass*

"The author is a great storyteller."

~ AstraDaemon

"Joslyn Chase skillfully connects subplots, then injects a few surprises, then connects things again in an interesting cycle; weave, disassemble, weave, repeat."

~ **Ron Keeler, Read 4 Fun**

"In the movie Field of Dreams, there is a now famous line, "If you build it, they will come." Apply this sentiment to Joslyn Chase--if she writes it, we will come and read it."

~ **William DeProspo, author of *Unlikely Outcome***

"Joslyn Chase paints intriguing pictures with vivid, colorful descriptions...you feel like you have a front row seat from which to watch as everything unfolds."

~ **Gabi Rosetti (reader, Amazon.com)**

"The flow of her writing is a delight to me, elegant and soothing, woven like fine linen."

~ **Margherita Crystal Lotus, author of *The Color Game***

CONTENTS

— · —

PROLOGUE

O N A CLEAR SUMMER day, the kind with a breeze that lifts the hair off your sweaty forehead and makes a tall glass of lemonade go down like an elixir of the gods, I think about the day I cheated Death.

I'd felt like such a lucky son of a gun. I hadn't an inkling that Death had marked me down in his little book and was coming back to claim his due. If I *had* known, I swear I'd have laid out the red carpet for him rather than have it happen like it did.

But on that July day, I was only twelve. I hadn't earned the perspective or wisdom that age and experience put on a person. I've had plenty of time between then and now to marvel over what happened that day and to speculate whether my moments going forward have been colored by those events in unexplained ways. As a man in my forties, I sometimes wonder if the setbacks, tragedies, and disappointments in my life were Death's way of garnishing my wages until he could collect in full.

As I remember that day, I'd woken and rolled lazily onto my back, staring at a ceiling painted bright by a band of dappled sunlight. Glinting motes floated on the air like a sprinkling of fairy dust and I pictured a magical day ahead, filled with barefoot wanderings, swimming holes, and stolen cookies.

A door slammed somewhere down the hallway and I guessed my older sister was getting an early start on her pouting and flouncing routine. I threw back the sheet and stripped off my pajamas, tossing them in a corner. As I zipped into a pair of jeans, the old staircase outside my room groaned, telling me mom had mounted the first few steps.

"Jay! Mandy! Breakfast!"

On the landing, the smell of bacon and pancakes greeted me, setting up a rumbling in my stomach. Dad had left already for the office, his chair empty, a syrup-smeared plate and half a glass of orange juice on the tablecloth in front of it.

"Don't forget to say grace, Jay," mom reminded, her back to me as she flipped another batch of pancakes.

Bowing my head, I said a quick and sincere prayer of thanks for bacon and long summer days before digging into the short stack on my plate. Just as the morning looked to be shaping into something glorious, mom turned from the counter and pointed the spatula at me.

"Chores today, kiddo. Downstairs bath, and clean your room. Honestly Jay, how do you find anything clean to wear in that mess?"

I kept my head lowered and hoped mom wouldn't notice the strawberry jam staining the front of my T-shirt. I tried to keep a whine out of my voice as I made my considered argument.

"Come on, mom. It's nice outside, but it might rain this afternoon. Can't I do my chores later?"

"Not a chance, dear one. You'll finish them before you go out to play."

I huffed a loud, long-suffering sigh, but mom only rolled her eyes and turned back to the stove. Starting in the bathroom, I scrubbed the sink, tub, and toilet, polished the mirror, and swept the floor.

After that, I headed up to my room, stomping on each step as a form of protest, and stared around at the heaps of dirty clothes, scattered game pieces, and old homework assignments discarded at random among the rest of the chaos.

Sorting clothes and shoes into one pile, toys into another, papers into a third, and making a fourth pile for everything else, I organized the mess. It didn't look any better.

Flopping onto my bed, I saw the band of light across the ceiling had moved, marking off the hours like a sundial as morning wasted toward afternoon. I crossed to the window and pushed it open, craning my neck to see the western sky. A disgruntled flare ruffled through my chest at the sight of creeping gray clouds, far off on the horizon.

Not fair.

Turning back to the piles, I stuffed the clothes into a hamper, shoved game pieces into boxes in my closet, and disposed of the rest of it as best I could without giving it too much thought. I wanted to get outside.

Running down the stairs, I passed mom folding laundry at the dining room table.

"Chores are done. I'm headed to Clint's."

"Hold it, Jay. You haven't cleaned the bathroom."

"Yes, I did."

"Your sister just finished cleaning the downstairs bathroom, so now you'll have to clean the one upstairs."

I stopped like I'd hit a stone wall, a wail of dissent rising up from the pit of my privations.

"I already cleaned the downstairs bathroom."

Mom made a sound with her tongue and placed a folded shirt on the top of a leaning stack. "I just saw Mandy wipe out the sink and put fresh towels on the racks, Jay. I haven't seen *you* in there this morning."

"You were washing dishes!" I pointed out, stung by this new injustice eating away more of my day. "You didn't see me, but I cleaned that bathroom first. All Mandy did was top it off."

Mom gave me a look. "Uh huh, not buying it, big guy. Upstairs, and I want that bathroom spic and span."

I looked up to see Mandy peering over the railing outside her bedroom. She smirked and turned away. The disgruntled flare inside me swelled and heated, touching my cheeks with a red-hot finger. I stared at my mother, calmly folding, impervious to my arguments, and I blew.

"You're not my jailer!" I shouted, thinking I'd heard something like that on a movie once. My feet stumbled forward of their own accord and I followed them, running out of the house and halfway down the street before my brain caught up with the rest of me.

Didn't matter. I wasn't going back, and I wasn't apologizing. I also wasn't going to Clint's where they'd be sure to find me if they came looking. I took off toward the greenbelt at the back of the neighborhood, on the far side of the lake.

A narrow swath of pines, oak, and eucalyptus flanked the rippled lake, which was really just an oversized trout pond kept stocked by the residents. A stiff breeze swayed the treetops, chilled by the approaching storm clouds, stirring the scent of pine and menthol.

Shivering, I wished I'd grabbed a windbreaker, but I would've frozen to death rather than go back for one now. My throat ached from the throb under my heart, and it hurt to swallow. Blinking hard, I turned my face into the wind and stared up at the top of my favorite climbing tree, a tall eucalyptus with long, narrow, silvery leaves.

The ground under my feet was hard and stony, covered by a thin carpet of dead and decaying leaves and pine needles. Bracing my foot against a rock embedded beneath the tree, I vaulted up and caught hold of the lowest branch, swinging my feet around it and clinging like a monkey.

I hung there for a moment, listening to the sound of my own breath chuffing against the silence of the wood. Then, pulling myself from branch to branch, I scrambled up the tree to the comfort of my "saddle," a place where I could straddle a wide bough and rest my head against the trunk.

Wrapping my arms around the peeling bark, I pressed my face into the strips. They felt like paper against my skin and smelled like chest rub. I tried to clear my mind, not to think about my ruined day or the consequences I'd have to face when I returned home.

A rumble of thunder, like a dog's warning growl, seemed to vibrate down through the trunk of the eucalyptus. How much shelter would these branches give me if it started to rain? The wind picked up strength and my perch swayed like the mast of a ship in swell.

Before I could decide to climb down, I heard running footsteps, and then a voice.

"Come on down, Jay!"

It was Clint. Squinting through the leaves, I saw he had his little brother, Zane, with him. I heard a skittering, like tiny feet running through the tops of the trees, and then the first raindrop hit me with a cold splat, dripping into my eye. A thousand brothers followed, pelting down fast.

Coming out of a tree is never as easy for me as climbing up. The rain soaked my hair, making it fall forward over my eyes and the bark grew slick with an oily moisture. Lowering myself from my saddle, I reached my toes toward the branch below. An enormous crack of thunder exploded above our heads, and I yelped.

My foot slipped at the same time I lost my grasp. Before I registered what had happened, I was falling to the stony ground below. My head hit rock, and the breath whooshed out of me like a spent balloon. My chest felt paralyzed and I couldn't pull in another lungful. I gawped like a landed fish.

Zane stood staring down at me. His face shone pale and his lips moved, but I heard no sound. Clint grabbed the boy, shaking him, shouting something before shoving him away. Zane disappeared.

Darkness closed in from the edges of my vision. I closed my eyes, but Clint knelt beside me and patted my cheeks.

"Oh no, buddy. No sleepytime for you. Stay with me."

My chest loosened and breath leaked into me in a pathetic wheeze, not enough to get behind the words I wanted to say. So tired now, I just wanted to go to sleep. I let my eyes fall shut.

Clint slapped my cheeks again, shocking me awake. "Buck up, Jay! We've got tadpoles to catch. And don't forget, we're building a hideout this summer. You're not going to make me do all the work myself, are you?"

I should have died that day, but a miracle kept me alive—a miracle by the name of Clint Fuller, my best friend, and—on any other day—my partner in climb.

One way and another, Clint badgered and bullied me into staying awake until the ambulance arrived. He saved my life that day.

It is my deepest regret that I wasn't able to do the same for him when his day came.

CHAPTER 1

— · —

THE WOMAN I MARRIED is not a nag.

I counted that as one of Vanessa's many qualities which made me a very lucky man. Until my luck changed, making up for the nagging I wasn't getting at home.

I heard the clack of businesslike, low heels in the hallway, and cringed. Why did the thought of this woman make me want to crawl under my desk? I forced a smile onto my face and waited for my new supervisor, Ms. Clapham, to poke her head in. She couldn't pass my office without stopping by to remind me about something I hadn't done yet.

"Hi, Jay." She held a steaming cup of coffee and blew on it with pursed lips as her gaze traveled around my office, no doubt cataloging deficits for future use. My space filled with the scent of her flowery coffee concoction, something fancy with bitter overtones. "Have you finished the sales copy for the Toliver account? I want to proof it before our presentation tomorrow."

"I'll have it on your desk by mid-afternoon."

She gave me a tight smile. "Make sure you do."

The heels clacked away, the sound vanishing as she turned into her carpeted office. I realized I was holding my breath and let it out in a slow dribble, like air escaping a leaky tire. I reached out my hand for a pencil and nearly knocked over the whole jar when the phone on my desk buzzed and lit up, jangling out the ringtone from *Top Gun*.

Clint.

I grinned down at the vibrating phone, knowing two things before I even picked up the call—I was about to get squeezed, and that whatever Clint wanted me to do, I'd go along with it.

Thirty-three years of life experience had washed under our bridge since that day under the eucalyptus trees, with Clint still bullying—his intentions pure—and me still complying—mostly to my great benefit. We were the best of friends, even separated by a thousand miles and a vast difference in lifestyle.

After college, I'd gone into advertising while Clint started up his own software development company designing animation programs and special effects generators for movies and television. He made his fortune three times over, sold the company, and devoted his life to indulging various passions.

Sometimes including me in his adventures.

I picked up the call, thinking I was prepared to hear anything Clint might throw my way.

I was wrong.

"The Lost Dutchman's Mine?" I ran a mental inventory, trying to remember the gist of the legend. "Clint, thousands of people have combed the Superstition Mountains looking for that mirage. It doesn't exist."

"It does, though, my friend. And I intend to uncover it."

"Why? I'm sure you'll have to turn anything you find over to the government."

"Naturally. It's not about the gold. It's about the thrill of the hunt. Come on, Jay—I'm making you an offer you can't resist."

"You always do."

I sighed, running a hand through what was left of my hair. "You said you'd pay me handsomely to come along. What, exactly, will you be paying me for? My charming company?"

"Of course, and I'd like you to manifest that charm by entertaining us around the campfire of an evening—a little song, a little dance, a little local folklore."

"What do you mean by 'us'? Who else have you conscripted?"

"We'll be a small party. Besides the two of us, there'll be just my brother, Zane, and the guides, Darren and Theta Halloway."

I hadn't seen Zane in years. I still remembered him as the freckle-faced pipsqueak who'd followed us around, always wanting in on whatever Clint was cooking up. I guess he was still at it.

"These guides—I assume they're the best money can buy?"

"Really, Jay—do you even need to ask? The Halloways run an outfitters and guide service out of Florence, Arizona and are well-versed in just about everything there is to know about the Superstitions—the mountains, as well as the myths."

"I'll bet she's pretty, too."

A brief silence opened up, letting me know I'd hit the target. Clint, once married and once divorced, had a weakness for good-looking women—especially when they wore another man's ring.

"How many times have you been out there already?" I asked.

"A couple. Had to scout things out, didn't I?"

I didn't relish the thought of stepping into a sticky situation. I wondered how well-established the flirtation was and thought about putting up a fight, but we both knew I wouldn't turn Clint down. What was the point in dragging it out?

"All right," I said, "but I've got to get the go-ahead from my boss, and I'm not hauling my guitar around that rough terrain."

"No," Clint agreed. "You've got a harmonica, don't you?"

"Yes," I admitted.

"And study up on the local legends. I want to be properly entertained."

"Okay, but Clint," I said, thinking about everything I knew of the Lost Dutchman's Mine, "what makes you think you can find the gold when no one else has?"

"Because I've got something none of them ever did."

"What is it?"

"Jump on a plane, Jay. I'll show you when you get here."

Chapter 2

I DROVE A RENTED Ford from the Phoenix airport, pursued by a succession of dust devils, little funnels of loose earth spinning beside the blacktop like wild dervishes. A growing anticipation swelled my chest as I thought about what might lay ahead, and curiosity over Clint's discovery hummed along with the car's motor, counting off the miles.

The Halloway ranch sprawled over a dusty bluff about four miles northwest of Florence, patterned in shades of gray and brown spangled by silvery green in the leaves of an olive grove and clusters of chaparral. A split rail fence meandered across the property, dividing it roughly into pastures occupied by livestock—horses, sheep, and a few cows.

Along the back side of the ranch, with occasional views of the Gila River, rested a series of log cabins, charmingly rustic in appearance while still providing most of the modern conveniences guests demand. Pulling into the parking area, I cut the motor and listened to it tick as it cooled.

A strange foreboding crept over me, prickling the skin at the back of my scalp. I found myself reluctant to open the car door, as if doing so would break some protective seal that held me safe inside the Ford.

Gripping the steering wheel in both hands, I squeezed, building the tension until my knuckles turned white. I held onto it, counting to ten, then let it go, feeling the tension drain away.

Ridiculous.

Popping the locks, I swung wide the car door, gasping a little at the blast of noonday heat. The monotonous coo of mourning doves played in the background like a bird lover's lullaby.

Grabbing my suitcase from the trunk, I squinted against the sun, trying to work out which cabin was mine. Clint had booked three cabins for the duration of our stay, even though we'd spend most nights up on the mountain. As I stood sweating, the door of cabin four flew open and Clint rushed out, grinning like a madman.

"Son of a gun, Jay. You made it."

"Was there ever any doubt?"

He hugged me around the shoulders and we slapped backs. The old feelings flooded over me and it was like we were kids again, setting out on an adventure.

He wore a red polo and jeans, and I saw with a little chagrin that he'd maintained his fitness level better than I had, still trim enough to wear the shirt tucked in and look good. Over the years, he'd managed to tame the cowlick in his head of dark hair and there were faint lines around his mouth and cobalt blue eyes, but essentially he was the boy I remembered.

"You're in five," Clint said, picking up my case. "I bet you're ready for a cold one."

The cabin looked like something out of a western movie, weathered boards and a wide, wrap-around veranda decked with rocking chairs. A wind chime hung from the rafters, tinkling out a melancholy tune.

"Does anyone actually sit out here in this heat?" I asked.

"Once the sun sinks behind those mountains, it chills right down most nights. You'll be surprised at the temperature swing."

Inside, I splashed my face with cool water and brushed the dust and grit out of my teeth. Denver was dry, but not like this, and I wasn't used to the sensation that my skin was shrinking on my bones. I patted my face with a thick, soft hand towel.

"Is Zane here yet?" I asked.

"In cabin three, taking a nap." He hesitated. "Which is fortunate because I wanted to talk to you alone."

"Uh-oh. What's Zane into now?"

"Trouble. As usual. He's not sharing any details with me, but he needs money."

"And you've got plenty to spare." I twisted the cap off a tiny bottle of lotion and dabbed some into my palm. It smelled like honeysuckle. "But you don't want to give him any."

"It's not that I don't want to give him any, Jay. It's just that I don't want to give him any *more*. I've handed him upwards of a million dollars over the past three years and he's got nothing to show for it. Just keeps asking for more. I don't think I'm doing him any favors."

"Time for some tough love?"

"Maybe," Clint said, his tone wistful. "Anyway, I plan to tell him his cash cow's gone dry."

"Thanks for the warning."

I rubbed the lotion over my reddened cheeks and forehead. "What's the story with the woman?" I asked, meeting Clint's eye in the mirror.

He shrugged. "Nothing to tell, really. She's a damn good guide, and a fine cook as well."

"Sounds like you're saying she'd make someone an excellent wife. Oh, wait. She *is* someone's wife."

"I know, Jay. I can't help it."

"I think I know what your problem is. You're so used to getting what you want that you have to want what you can't have."

He looked dejected, and I took pity on him, counting the blessing of my own excellent wife as more valuable than all the money in Clint's bank account.

"Is the husband the jealous type? Did you bring me here to back you in a fist fight on the desert trail?"

Clint grimaced. "The husband's a decent guy. I'm trying to behave myself, Jay. I brought you along to help me do that."

I screwed the cap on the lotion bottle and tossed it into the wicker basket on the bathroom counter, a long slab of desert granite, polished to a wicked shine. "Fair enough. Now show me what you promised—the secret to The Lost Dutchman's Mine."

"Let's go talk in my cabin."

"You got beer in your cabin?"

"On ice."

"Lead the way."

As we clomped across the wooden veranda, a man spoke from behind us. We turned and Clint said, "Jay, this is Darren Hallo—"

Before he could get the name out, the big man barreled toward me, jaw squared in a grim scowl, swinging his arm like a club in an open-handed slap.

The blow connected with my shoulder and sent me stumbling.

I hit the rail.

CHAPTER 3

— · —

"WHAT THE—"

The porch rail bit into my ribcage, but I managed to catch myself before I toppled, stunned by the sudden, unprovoked attack. Clint had Darren Halloway up against the wall of the cabin, a fistful of the man's shirt clenched in his hand, teeth bared like a slavering dog. The sorrowful cooing of the doves continued in the background, a Greek chorus for our hot little drama.

"Whoa, easy man," Darren said, raising and showing his empty hands like this was a bank stickup. "I'm sorry to strike out like that, but there was no time to warn you."

Clint relaxed his hold, and I straightened, stepping under the lip of the roof to get my first good look at the man. Out of the sun's glare, I saw that he was well-muscled but softening with age, with sandy hair, and a slightly stubbled chin. He turned to me, his expression apologetic, hand extended to shake mine.

"I had to kill the sucker before she got her stinger into you."

I stared, confused, my stunned brain trying to connect the dots between his words after what Clint had just told me about his wife. Was the man somehow referring to her?

"What are you talking about?" Clint said.

Darren stooped over the planks of the veranda floor, lifting something carefully into his hand. He held it out for us to see. An enormous black insect, like an ant queen with orange wings, spanned nearly the entire width of his sizable palm. He pointed out the wicked-looking stinger.

"Tarantula hawk," he explained. "It was fixing to perch on your shoulder. One zap from this little lady will give you the worst three minutes of your life. The pain is instant, excruciating, and totally debilitating."

Oh, *that* she. I stared at the creature, suddenly glad he'd knocked me sideways. "Are you sure she's dead?"

Darren dropped the insect to the boards and pulverized it under his boot. "She is now."

I felt sick. "Is it a wasp?" I asked.

"Yes, one of the largest and most aggressive."

I happened to know a few things about wasps. Unlike bees, wasps do not die after one sting. They can go after you again and again.

Clint turned to me, his face going pale. "Jay's allergic to stings," he told Darren.

"Do you have an EpiPen?" the guide asked.

I nodded.

"Keep it handy."

Clint shuddered. "Where there's one, aren't there likely to be more?"

Darren shoved his hands into the back pockets of his jeans and looked around, squinting against the sun. "I'll have my foreman check it out. If there's a nest on the property he'll find and destroy it."

He held his hand out again and this time I shook it gratefully. "Darren Halloway," he said. "Good to meet you, Jay. Clint's told me what a fine friend you are. I hope you'll be mine, as well."

I nodded, but before I could speak, he continued. "I won't hold you up. I know you've got a lot to talk about. I just came to say dinner's at six tonight so we can turn in early. We leave at dawn."

"Sounds good, Darren. See you then."

I looked again at the pulpy remains of the squashed insect and grimaced. Clint gave my shoulder a light punch. "Welcome to Arizona. I've been here for four days without a hitch. You arrive and create a stir in the first five minutes. How do you do it?"

"Rare talent, I suppose."

"Well come on, Mr. Talent. There's more excitement to come."

He strode toward his cabin, an eagerness vibrating off him that spread to me as I trotted behind him. I couldn't help the grin that spread across my face, and I felt the same boyhood pull of adventure that I had so many times before with Clint.

"How much do you know about Jacob Waltz?" he asked as he held the door open for me to enter.

"The Dutchman?"

"Right. The German man they dubbed the Dutchman."

The air conditioning was a blessed relief, even after our short jaunt between cabins. Glancing around, I saw the room was decorated with the same kind of rustic opulence as my own—oil paintings of desert landscapes, rich, polished wood, eiderdown on the bed I glimpsed through a doorway, and a bearskin rug in front of the fireplace. At the cabin's rear, an enormous wall of thick, double-paned glass gave a spectacular view of the valley, shaded by an awning to deflect the heat.

Clint's cabin, though, had something mine didn't. The center of the living space was interrupted by a glass cube forming an atrium, open to the sky. A sliding door allowed access to a small garden of cacti and succulents with a unique bench of sculpted and varnished wood, perfect for moments of meditation.

As I stood admiring it, Clint asked again, "What do you know about the Dutchman?"

Turning from the atrium, I sank into a deep armchair, propping my feet on a leather ottoman. "I know he really did find gold in them thar hills," I said, "but died before he successfully passed on the location."

Clint nodded. "That's the way the legend runs." He opened a fridge in the wet bar and pulled out two golden bottles of Modelo, popping the tops.

"Glass or bottle?"

"Bottle's fine."

He handed mine over and propped himself on the arm of my chair, tipping back a generous portion of his own bottle before continuing.

"There are all kinds of rumors," he said, wiping his mouth with the back of a sunburnt hand. "But let's stick to substantiated fact for a moment. Toward the end, Jacob took sick with pneumonia and was nursed by a woman named Julia Thomas. He never recovered, but before he died, he told Julia he had gold from the mine stashed in a box under his bed. He'd been living off it for years."

"Honoring the age-old tradition of keeping your money under your mattress."

"So it seems. Julia and a fellow called Rhinehart Petrasch checked out the old man's story and saw it was true. There was ore in that box. Rich ore. Rhinehart went back and told Jacob it must have come from an isolated pocket but Jacob said no, it's a vein, with enough in sight to make millionaires out of twenty men."

I whistled. "That was back in the 1890's wasn't it? The price of gold is a lot higher now than it was back then. Assuming Waltz spoke the truth, and figuring in the rate of inflation, it would probably make millionaires out of a hundred men or more by now."

"Could be, Jay. Could be."

Clint's voice had gone soft. He stared out through the expanse of glass, past the scrub and scattered saguaro, to the jutting mountains in the distance. His eyes shone, glinting in the reflection off the window, or perhaps lit by some inner source.

He cleared his throat, turning away from the view. "So Jacob started telling Julia and Rhinehart how to find the mine. He said to take the trail in from the northwest corner of the Superstition Mountains. He told them the setting sun shone into the entrance of the mine, glittering on the gold, so they figured it had to face west."

I nodded, entranced by that vision of sunlight burnishing golden stones, making them shine.

"He gave a lot of other instructions about which gorge to take, which direction to go, which landmarks to look for, but there are doubts about whether Julia and Rhinehart recorded it correctly. One line of thought is that they were celebrating so hard over their anticipated fortune that they failed to pay proper attention."

"Due to drink, you mean?"

"Or sheer euphoria. At any rate, after Jacob passed, Julia cashed in everything she owned to provision their expedition into the mountain to find the mine. She was accompanied by Rhinehart and his brother, Hermann."

Clint gave a dry chuckle and downed another third of his bottle.

"They picked the wrong time of year to be going up there. After searching for weeks in the summer sun, they returned depleted and defeated. Julia was destitute, and never went back to the mountain."

"And the two brothers?"

"They quarreled, parted company. But one way or another, both of them spent the rest of their lives looking for that gold."

Clint's empty bottle made a musical sound as he placed it on the polished surface of the dining table. Reaching into a case that rested beneath, he brought out a large volume, and with gentle care laid it on the table before him. Its cracked leather cover and yellowing pages released a musty smell into the room, giving me an urge to sneeze.

"Julia ended up with most of Jacob's earthly possessions, though she sold much of it in an effort to keep afloat after her failure to find the gold. I traced this item and bought it at auction last month. It's a German Bible that belonged to Jacob Waltz."

So this was his big reveal. I couldn't keep the disappointment from my face. "Come on, Clint. Surely thousands have searched that Bible for clues to the mine's location. Without success."

"True," Clint agreed, "but I don't see how that impacts me. *I* own it now."

16

He walked to the fridge and popped the top off another bottle. After a long swallow, he held the bottle to the light and examined its golden glow, letting out a satisfied grunt. He turned to me and winked.

"Let me tell you about what I've found."

CHAPTER 4

—·—

THE SMILE ON HIS face was the same one he'd worn thirty years ago when he'd guided me through the woods to an abandoned camper full of moth-eaten pillows and pulp fiction paperbacks. We'd hung out in that metal hulk until the weather turned too cold to make it fun. In the spring when we'd returned, the camper was gone.

"Have a seat over here, Jay," he said, inviting me to join him at the table. Heaving myself up from the padded armchair, I obeyed.

"I hadn't figured Jacob Waltz for a religious man," he said, leaning forward, "but there are several scriptural passages marked in these pages, seemingly at random, with handwritten notes in the margins. Like everyone else, I read through them with great anticipation, but there are hundreds of them and no way to tell their significance."

He paused. "Or so I thought."

I perked up a little. Clint had always been a lucky son of a gun, fortune smiling on him where others got nothing but gloom. "You saw something everyone else missed."

He gave me a wide smile. "I'm a Sunday School graduate, remember? We used to follow what we called scripture chains, going from one cross-referenced verse to another. Now, this Bible is old. It doesn't contain footnotes, *and* it's in German, so this was not easy, but I found a scripture chain. And I followed it."

Impatience welled in me. "And where did it lead?"

"It led me on a treasure hunt."

He pushed the book toward me. "Do you see this symbol?" He pointed to a tiny hand-printed mark that looked like a ladybug. "It's small, almost unnoticeable, and has probably faded away in some instances, but the passages marked with such a symbol have another reference written in the margin beside them. That's the chain, buddy."

A bubble of excitement rose within me, fizzing in my chest.

"I'm sure I missed some links, but I found enough, Jay. I found enough."

He pulled the Bible to him and gently turned the pages until he reached the scripture he was looking for. He had a notepad beside him. "I used an English Bible to translate. The first verse I found marked by that symbol was Matthew 13:44:

"Again, the kingdom of heaven is like unto treasure hid in a field; the which when a man hath found, he hideth, and for joy thereof goeth and selleth all that he hath, and buyeth that field."

"Easy to see the significance in that," I said.

"Right, and the reference in the margin led me to Ezekiel 43:1:

"Afterward he brought me to the gate, even the gate that looketh toward the east."

"Toward the east? I thought the mine was somewhere in the northwest region of the mountains, with its mouth facing west."

"So does everyone else. That's what Jacob told Julia, on his deathbed. But the scripture written in the margin is Isaiah 24:16, which says:

"From the uttermost part of the earth have we heard songs, even glory to the righteous. But I said, My leanness, my leanness, woe unto me! the treacherous dealers have dealt treacherously; yea, the treacherous dealers have dealt very treacherously."

I thought about it. "The uttermost part of the earth sounds like it could be a reference to the mine. But who are the treacherous dealers, and what does it mean?"

"I'll show you what I think it means in a minute, but first let's follow to the next scripture, Psalm 51:6:

"Behold, thou desirest truth in the inward parts: and in the hidden part thou shalt make me to know wisdom."

Clint looked at me, a delighted grin breaking across his face. "I decided to look in the inward parts of this book. I used steam to loosen the glue and using the *utmost* care, I peeled the lining away from the back cover and found these."

He showed me two sheets of thin, yellowed paper sandwiched between clear protective sleeves designed to preserve them from further decay. The first was a letter written in a spiky hand, the sepia ink faded so that it was indecipherable in some spots. It read:

To the man of God who finds this,

Those with their hearts set on treasure deal with me kindly because I hold the key. But they are wolves in sheep's clothing. I will reveal (faded) treachery to me, I repay with treachery. Only one who seeks with pure intent will find truth. All others are led astray. (Faded) the room you will see the pillar of rock and the stones which must be (faded) the hidden entrance.

Would I could be with you to direct you aright. I fear without my guiding hand, no man shall ever see the gold, and perhaps that is best. There are spirits there, who (faded) and wrath upon the unwary. Beware, and tread with integrity, for where your treasure is, there will your heart be also.

Jacob Waltz, 1891

"Justified or not, I think Jacob Waltz believed Julia and Rhinehart meant to betray him. So he lied."

I sat stunned. My friend really had found something no other seeker had accessed. Two things.

The other protective sleeve contained a map.

CHAPTER 5

— · —

T HE SUN TREMBLED ON the cusp of rising as we reached the mouth of the canyon, trickling a watery, lemon-yellow radiance into a late September morning laced with a hint of chill.

The subdued call of the ever-present mourning dove reached me from their nests in the sparse mesquite and cottonwoods as they woke to the new day and began foraging for seeds and berries. Too early for people talk, theirs was the only conversation mingling with the clop of hooves on the desert sand as we entered the opening.

I straightened in the saddle, feeling energy awake in my body as the day grew in vigor. Leaning forward, I patted my horse, a good-tempered Appaloosa named Sandia, and she tossed her head, sending the plumes of her mane tumbling against her spotted neck. Sage and horse dung scented the air as I pulled the reins gently left, guiding Sandia to follow Clint's bay mare.

Theta Halloway took the lead, and it was easy to understand Clint's attraction to her. Long, chestnut hair cascaded from beneath her Stetson to bounce against the back of her checked shirt. I shifted my eyes away from the view of her shape filling the saddle and reminded myself I was a happily married man who wanted to return to my wife with a light heart and no regrets.

Theta had a natural charm and exuded confidence, but in no way came across as a coquette. I was relieved. I had not wanted to be witness to a flirtatious drama, and she gave no indication she had such an agenda. Clint's behavior was circumspect, as well, though I imagined he was enjoying the view of which I deprived myself.

Little brother, Zane, fell in behind me, and Darren Halloway brought up the rear, along with three heavy-laden pack mules. As we progressed into a canyon on the southeastern side of the Superstitions, the passage narrowed, cutting off the sun's rays, painting shades of purple and gray in the shadows. The comfortable tranquility of our journey continued, each of us enjoying the morning in our own way, accompanied only by gentle horse music, the occasional swishing of a long-haired tail, a brief whinnied comment.

As I settled into the rhythm of Sandia's walk, listening to the sound of the horse's hooves against the stone-scattered floor of the gorge, it seemed to me suddenly like the ticking of a fateful clock, carrying us forward in time. With a mixture of anticipation and queer, undefined dread, I wondered what events awaited.

At length, we reached a wider spot and Theta pulled up, waiting for the rest of us to gather round.

"Let's rest for a bit," she said, swinging down from her mare. "Make sure you stay hydrated. Why don't you take a drink while I regale you with some local history."

I climbed out of the saddle and screwed the top off my canteen, tipping a mouthful of cool water down my throat.

"Keep in mind that nothing I tell you is hard and fast," Theta warned. "Just bits and pieces that have survived the years."

She took a sip from her own canteen, capped it, and swept an arm to encompass the breadth of the canyon. "These mountains were an Apache stronghold in the 1800's. A family by the name of Peralta came up from northern Mexico and developed a productive mine somewhere in this vicinity about mid-century. Their last expedition to carry gold back to Mexico happened in 1848. As the story goes, their party was attacked by Apaches and massacred, except for a few who managed to escape and return to Mexico."

She looked past us to the cliff walls and I followed her gaze, seeing nothing beyond seamed and pockmarked stone, lit by the creeping sun.

"You all are here," she said, "because of Jacob Waltz. It's believed that Jacob located the mine with the help of a Peralta family descendant and worked it with his partner, Jacob Weiser, allegedly hiding one or more caches of gold in these mountains."

"Do *you* believe it's here, Theta?" Zane asked, his tone sardonic, matching his raised eyebrows and thrusting chin.

Darren laughed. "Oh, there's plenty of gold in this canyon," he assured them. "It comes from people like you paying people like us."

Clint grinned, and held his canteen up in a toast. "I'll drink to that."

We all joined in, raising our canteens and swallowing more water as Theta continued.

"Apaches struck again, and Weiser was fatally wounded. Or so the story goes. Some believe Jacob Waltz murdered his partner."

She paused. "One thing is certain--gold fever does strange things to people. Darren and I have witnessed some disturbing behavior while guiding folks through these mountains. I hope I won't be seeing anything like that on this expedition."

Our dutiful chuckles echoed slightly in the stone passage. She'd clearly meant it as humor, but her words held a hint of warning, as well.

I shivered as we pressed on, moving deeper into the shadowed gorge, but soon the sun had risen enough to radiate against the canyon walls, heating the air and bringing out a ring of sweat along my hairline.

After another hour of clopping through the narrow passage, the canyon walls angled away, opening out into an area of sandy, scrub-covered hills and craggy rocks. The trail became less-defined, often disappearing entirely, but Theta never faltered in her lead.

The horses followed without complaint, but I had to work to quell the little swellings of doubt. I thought about how vulnerable we were out here, isolated in a land untamed by modern considerations, far from cell service and supermarkets.

We approached an unusual rock formation, a tall, flattened spire, curving slightly forward so that it looked like a petrified wave rising up from the desert floor. A scattering of smaller rocks lay in the small shadow cast by the near noonday sun.

Theta pulled up and dismounted. "This is a good spot for lunch."

Each of our horses was weighed down with saddlebags containing water, food, and supplies, and the pack mules carried additional equipment. Darren and Theta passed out boxed lunches and cold drinks, and we perched on rocks, eating in the shrinking shade of the stony wave.

Shooing away a persistent fly, I finished my sandwich and started on a home-baked chocolate chip cookie as big as the palm of my hand. Buttery and delicious, the chips just starting to melt in the desert heat, it hit the spot.

I noticed Clint staring around at the landscape, an excited look on his face. As I swallowed my last bite, he drew my attention ahead, to where rock walls rose again, marking the mouth of another gorge.

"Do you see them?" he asked. "The cliff dwellings?"

I squinted my eyes against the sun and peered where he gestured. The noonday glare played tricks with my vision, carving shadows into the rock wall, but when I shaded my gaze and focused on the spot, they were still there.

"They're not a mirage," Darren said. "I knew you'd be interested in those caves."

Clint looked at me, lowering his voice. "I think those are the ones Jacob marked on the map. Hot damn! We're on the right track, Jay."

CHAPTER 6

— · —

A STIR OF EXCITEMENT fluttered in my chest. I had to admit I was not immune to Clint's gold fever. The thought of finding the elusive vein of ore sought so long, by so many, was intoxicating.

Clint turned to Darren. "I'm definitely interested," he said. "Can we take a little time to look around?"

"You're paying for the time, so you get to choose how we spend it. I reckon we can spare an hour or two and still get to the campsite before dark."

He cocked his head at Theta, and she nodded. "One of us had better go with you," she said. "There are a few hazards to watch out for."

Leaving Darren to clear up after lunch, Theta and Zane set out with Clint and me, the desert gravel crunching under out boots as we trudged along the trace of a path to the cliff dwellings.

"We warned you about snakes and scorpions before we left the ranch," Theta said, "but some of those caves are deep enough to house bats. And where there are bats, there's guano. The smell of the stuff will knock you flat and if you step in a fresh batch, you can bid your boots goodbye. The real problem, though, is the dried residue. If you stir it up and breathe the dust, it can cause issues."

"Let's steer clear of the bat caves," Clint said. "But can we get a closer look at some of these more shallow depressions? Like that one."

He pointed to a sunken place in the cliff wall, like a giant's thumb print. The remains of a mud brick wall stretched halfway across the entrance, and I felt a stir of fascination, a sudden curiosity about the people who'd lived here, in this harsh environment, so long ago.

"Sure," Theta said. "That one's easy enough to get to, but we need to be careful. These dwellings are ancient, and this is all that's left of them. They should be studied and enjoyed, but they should also be preserved. Please watch where you step, and don't touch the wood. It's very fragile."

The depression was only about a dozen yards above the desert floor, and a formation of rocks at the base of the cliff gave us a boost, making it easy to climb the remaining few feet. I pulled myself onto the lip of the shallow cave and stared through the doorway of the adobe hut. I thought something moved there, but when I drew closer, I saw nothing but a sandy floor, littered with broken twigs.

A slight shiver worked down my spine. An ancient people had lived here, cooked their dinners, birthed their children, rested their bones. And somewhere, not too far away, their bones must lie. Did their restless spirits haunt this place? Legend says they do.

Clint stood beside me. "I feel it, too. The years weigh heavy here."

Behind us, Zane and Theta moved apart and the light shifted, allowing a wash of sunshine to penetrate the shadows. I stooped down, getting a closer look at the adobe blocks forming a ragged wall around the sand-floored room.

"Look, you can see finger marks in the bricks." Amazed, I fitted my own hand against the grooves made so long ago, wondering if it might transport me back in time, like in *Outlander*. Of course it didn't, and I stepped back to let the others see.

As I stared around me, my imagination sketched life and details into the shell of a house. "There must have been *things* here," I said. "Like arrowheads and bows. Blankets, dishes. Those things women used to grind corn."

"Metates," Theta supplied, "but anything like that has long since disappeared."

We spent another ten minutes in the shallow cave, looking and thinking, musing over ancient people long gone.

"I'm heading back," Zane said, kneeling to lower himself over the edge. I followed, but just before my head sunk below eye level, I caught a glimpse of Clint and Theta, standing close, his hand reaching for hers. She didn't pull away.

I cleared my throat and stretched out a foot, seeking a toehold below. I remembered my tree-climbing days with Clint, how it had always been easier going up than coming down. That hadn't changed.

I lost my grip on the jagged stone and fell to the platform of rock below, twisting my ankle on the landing.

Theta looked down from the lip of the depression. "Are you all right?" she called.

Wincing, I moved my foot in a careful circle. Tender, but completely mobile.

"I'm fine. Just landed wrong on my ankle."

She and Clint climbed down and Theta knelt beside me, satisfying herself the injury was minor.

"We have a cold pack we can put on that ankle." Hefting me up, she pushed herself under my shoulder, like a crutch. Clint took the other side. "Let's get you back on a horse."

After seeing me settled in the saddle with a chemical cold pack shoved down my boot, Darren led our caravan into the mouth of another gorge, Theta trailing behind to make sure no one fell by the wayside. We clopped along in sleepy silence, and I began to understand the attractions of a Mexican siesta as I fought to keep my eyes from drooping shut.

In the late afternoon, we reached a flat, clear spot against the canyon wall, with an overhang that provided a sort of natural ramada. Darren hopped off his horse and began removing saddlebags.

"This is where we camp for the night."

Both Halloways turned down our offers of help.

"You three should rest," Darren said. "You're not used to this heat, and this is what you pay us for."

"I guess I'm shelling out enough to make it worth your while," Clint said.

"Damn straight." Darren shot Clint a grin as he tossed a bundled tent onto the canyon floor, sending up a flurry of dust. "Camp chairs are over there."

Dusk fell fast, casting long, eerie shadows against the screen of stone as the Halloways moved about their tasks. I eased back in my canvas chair, my foot propped up and covered with another cold pack. I breathed in the smoky scent of campfire and horses.

"Brings back some memories, don't it?" Clint said, gazing up into the indigo ceiling where the first stars were winking into sight.

"For me it does," Zane said. "At least on those times you let me tag along."

"Which was most every time, little brother."

"That's the way you remember it, but I remember different."

Clint sighed and said nothing. We stretched out and listened to the crackling fire. After a full day in the saddle, my aching hips and thighs hurt worse than my ankle. I didn't know if a night of sleeping on the ground would help or make it worse. Much as I hated to face the thought, I was no longer the young boy of Clint's fond memories.

Theta served us plates of charbroiled steaks with cowboy beans, hot rolls, and corn on the cob. I contemplated asking for seconds, but the smell of apple cobbler bubbling in a dutch oven tucked among the coals convinced me to save some room.

As I scraped the last of the sugared apples from my plate, Clint said. "I think it's about time you broke out the harmonica, Jay."

"How about a story instead?" I asked. "I've got one I've been waiting to tell."

"Fair enough. Give us your once upon a time."

CHAPTER 7

— • —

A LOG ON THE flames shifted and popped, sending up a plume of sparks. Coughing, I fanned smoke away from my face and repositioned my sore foot on the camp stool. In the distance, I heard the yipping of coyotes, a feral, lonely sound, and I was glad of good company and a bright fire.

Tipping my head, I wet my whistle in preparation for telling my story, the beer no longer cold, and going flat. I finished the bottle and Theta brought me a new one as she came through, collecting empty plates. Her long hair swirled around her shoulders as she stooped and turned, and the fire teased red highlights from it, glinting like rubies. Mesmerizing.

Clint followed her with his eyes, his gaze wistful and hungry. I needed to do my job and get his mind off her. Putting some energy into my voice, I began spinning my tale.

"The Wild West suffered a crime wave back in the late 1800s. Train robbery was coming into fashion. It seemed like everybody was doing it, so New Mexico passed a law, making it a capital crime. Suddenly, Arizona looked a lot more attractive to a train robber wanting to dodge the death penalty."

"That's right," Zane said, holding his bottle high. "Go where the opportunity is."

"You would have fit right in, Zane," I told him. "So, robbers tended to wait until the train crossed the border into Arizona before making their move, and people in Arizona figured they ought to do something about it. So they passed a similar law, making train robbery a hanging crime.

"Unfortunately, things didn't work out the way they expected. You see, this was the golden age of the gentleman train robber. No muss, no fuss, and no one hurt, was the blueprint of the day. The robbers tended to be courteous, even romantic figures, and juries just wouldn't convict when no one was injured or killed during the robbery. Not if it meant hanging."

"A lot of criminals going scott free, were there?" Clint asked, a hint of amusement in his voice.

Relieved to see I had his attention, I leaned forward, starting to enjoy myself.

"There were," I agreed. "Although one such robber was not so lucky. Caught and convicted, Black Jack Ketchum swung from the gallows. The hangman made some kind of miscalculation and Black Jack's head rolled. Literally. That might be partly why all the states in the West dropped the death penalty for train robbery soon after."

"Leaving the way open again, for aspiring train robbers," Clint added.

"Exactly. Some of them had it down to a science. They simply held up the train, ordered the engine car detached, along with the express car containing the safe, and rolled it off to a siding where they'd blow open the safe and ride off with the takings."

Zane let out a belch and patted his stomach. "Sounds like easy money."

"That's what Joe George and Grant Wheeler were thinking when they decided to try their hand at it. A couple of cowboys looking to make a fast buck. They bought a load of dynamite at the local hardware store and to explain their purchase, they spread the word they were taking up mining."

I grinned and shook my head. "Those boys didn't know the first thing about mining. Or dynamite. Their plan started out fine. They stashed the dynamite and their getaway horses near a siding, pulled their pistols, and held up the train."

"Oh sure," Clint laughed. "What could go wrong?"

"That's what they thought. So, they haul the engine and the express car off to the siding, and when they open it up, Joe and Grant get real excited. Nine bags of silver pesos lay stacked beside the safe. The cowboys figure if they're leaving all that silver just laying around outside, the safe must be jam-packed with the good stuff.

"So they cram a few sticks of dynamite around the door of the safe, light the fuse, and run for cover. After the explosion, they hurry to the express car and see the safe sitting there, just as tight and pretty as it ever was."

I paused to pull a swig from my beer bottle, gratified to see both Clint and Zane rapt and waiting. The clank of pots and pans reached me from beyond our improvised fire pit, as Darren and Theta finished up the evening chores.

"So they try it again," I continued. "They shove a few more sticks of dynamite around the door of the safe, light it, and run. Another explosion. Another disappointment. The safe door is still secure."

"Sounds like the two of them should've stayed on the ranch," Clint said, laughing.

Zane shot him a sour look. "Sometimes things on the ranch don't work out. Sometimes you need a boost, a break, a little help."

Clint leaned forward, placing a hand on Zane's knee. "I've given you more than a little help, bro. I'm thinking I gave you too much."

The air thickened with sudden tension. Zane shoved at Clint's hand, his face twisting in a sneer as he drew breath for a reply. Before he could speak, I held up a hand and cleared my throat with emphasis, hoping to steer off the storm. "Hey, give me a break. I'm trying to tell a story here."

Zane stood. His face glowed orange with anger, dancing flames reflected in his eyes. Stepping into my personal space, he gave me a hard look, a vein near his hairline pulsing like a writhing snake.

"I don't give a damn about your story."

CHAPTER 8

— • —

S TALKING INTO THE DARKNESS, Zane passed Darren and Theta as they came to sit by the fire, ignoring their inquiring looks. As the Halloways stepped into the glow of the dwindling flames, Theta raised her eyebrows, nodding in Zane's direction. Clint and I both shrugged.

She pulled one of the camp chairs closer to Clint.

"At any rate," she said, "*I* want to hear your story."

"No need to start from the beginning," Darren added. "We've heard them all before."

"Great." I settled in my chair, hoping I could pull Clint back into the thread of the narrative and keep him from worrying about his brother or mooning over the woman at his side.

"By now, Joe and Grant are getting a little desperate," I began.

"Oh! I like this one," Theta said, smiling approvingly.

"So they pack more dynamite around the door of the safe and this time, they cover it with the bags of pesos to provide ballast and direct the force of the explosion. They light the fuses and hightail it for cover.

"Ka-boom! The huge explosion blows the express car to bits, blasting the pesos into the sky like shrapnel. And the safe..."

I paused, willing to let one of the others steal my thunder.

"...was empty," Clint finished.

"Yes! Well, more or less. There wasn't much in there, and the failed train robbers don't have time to hunt up all the pieces of silver they've blasted to kingdom come. They get on their horses and ride."

Theta hid a smile and nodded at me to go on.

"So the sheriff tries to put together a posse to round them up, but no one volunteers. By now, the news is out about what happened, and every able-bodied citizen is out in the desert with a rake, gathering up the scattered pesos."

Darren laughed. "And here's the funniest part," he said. "A month later, they did the whole thing again. Same train, same crew, same procedure."

"Only this time," Theta said, "the order of the train cars had been switched, so they ended up with the mail car instead of the express car containing the safe."

"That's when they gave up and left town for good," I said.

I didn't want to tell the rest of the story, how those two foolish cowboys ended up in an early grave. I hoped to end the evening on a light and comic note. Pulling the harmonica from my pocket, I drew breath to play, but Darren spoke, and something in his quiet tone made me put the instrument away.

"There's an old Indian story about this canyon. They say in the beginning, when everything was new, the sun introduced the sky to the wind, and they played together in the great expanse."

Darren crouched over the fire, stirring it with a stick. I watched, mesmerized, as sparks leapt into the darkness and disappeared. A shadowy figure materialized and dropped silently into the chair beside Clint as Zane rejoined us.

"Now, with the passage of centuries filled with wars, illness, and hard times," Darren continued, "there are many uneasy dead within these stone walls. The old-timers say that when the sun hides and the sky becomes dark, the wind blows through the canyon, calling to the dead. And the dead answer."

We all listened, but the air was still.

"No ghosts out tonight," Clint commented.

"You're wrong about that," Zane said. Firelight limned his face, casting strange shadows beneath his eyes, and his voice was solemn. "I'm sorry about earlier. Blame it on the long day, or the blasted heat. But I've got to tell you—this place is full of spirits, and they're not happy to see us here. The legend of the Lost Dutchman has great entertainment value, but I did some digging for the story behind the story. And it's not pretty."

Clint made an impatient gesture and I watched the muscles around his mouth tighten. "What are you talking about, Zane?"

"After copper was discovered in these mountains, greedy prospectors started invading, looking for more ore, stealing the land and scarring the landscape. Some think Apache spirits used the legend of the gold mine to lure these grasping treasure hunters to their deaths. Every year, a number of seekers and hikers disappear in these canyons and many times, the bodies are never found."

I leaned forward. "Are you suggesting the mine is cursed, like the tombs of the pharaohs? Death to all who enter here?"

"I'm suggesting there never *was* a mine. I think Jacob Waltz made a deal with the dead. His side of the bargain was to lure prospectors in—a blood sacrifice to the Apache spirits. And they rewarded him with gold."

Clint laughed. A dry, humorless sound. The Halloways rose, disappearing into their tent without a word, opting to stay out of it.

"Then why are you here, little brother?" Clint asked.

"I came along because I'm worried about you. Your obsession with the mine—"

"I'm not obsessed. Just determined."

"Call it what you want. I fear for you, Clint. We should leave here. Tomorrow."

"Go if you want to, Bro. I'm pressing on."

Zane sighed, and pushed himself to the edge of his chair. "If you're going, I'm going." He stood. "G'night."

Shoulders slumped, head down, Zane wandered back to his tent. I looked at Clint, thought about saying something, but those muscles around his mouth were still taut and I knew it wouldn't be productive.

"I'm beat," I said. "Heading for bed."

He nodded a goodnight, but his gaze never left the flickering fire. As I unzipped the flap of my tent, I thought I heard something moving in the darkness beyond the camp site. Straining my ears and eyes, I tried to discern more, but came up empty. I stepped inside the tent, leaving the flap open. It was dark, but the fire's glow through the canvas was enough for me to undress by.

When I'd finished, I zipped shut the flap and reached to turn down the lip of my sleeping bag, glimpsing something dark against the white of my pillowcase. Rummaging through my backpack, I found a flashlight and focused the beam at the head of my sleeping bag.

A ribbon of ice traced up my spine as I stared at the doll. It leered back from the pillow, a rictus grin on its face. Dressed in a sort of beaded buckskin, the features were crudely sewn into the fabric face with coarse black thread. A strip of yarn formed a headband around a fringe of hair, and a few sparse whiskers had been drawn on with a marker.

Crude as it was, the doll bore me an unmistakable resemblance, capturing some of the details of my clothing and appearance. Disturbing in the extreme, after those ghost stories around the campfire. But as I lifted the doll and turned it over, one thing above all chilled my blood.

A jagged shard of sharpened stone protruded from the doll's back.

CHAPTER 9

— · —

I DIDN'T FEEL I'D slept much, but a groggy sensation, like climbing up out of a well, told me I'd been deeper than I thought. I lay in my sleeping bag, staring at the doll I'd thrown aside last night. It sprawled against the curved, olive green side of the tent, legs pointing in opposite directions. I picked it up and looked at the stone dagger still embedded in its rag-stuffed heart. A tiny tuft of downy feather fluttered in the wake of my breath, attached somehow to the end of the spike, and I realized what the shaft represented.

The doll had been shot in the back with a stone arrow.

The smell of coffee and sausages permeated my tent, and I knew it was time to get going. Glaring at the doll, I crawled from my sleeping bag and pulled on the same pair of jeans I'd worn yesterday, feeling for the cylindrical shape of the EpiPen I'd kept in my pocket since the day I'd arrived. I added a clean shirt and took a few steps to test my ankle, finding it nearly good as new.

I knelt on the floor of the tent and sent up a quick prayer of thanks.

Poking my head from the tent, I saw a heavy layer of gray hovering over the campsite, bringing with it a smell like a wet screen door. It spoke of rain--either to come, or fallen and gone, and I counted our natural stone roof as a boon.

The other four had already gathered around the newly-lit fire, murmuring their good mornings as I joined them.

"Which one of you thought this was funny?" I asked, holding up the doll.

They passed it around, each looking mystified. "Where'd you get it?" Clint asked.

"It was someone's idea of a pillow mint." I looked around at the four of them. "Come on, own up. It had to be one of you, right?"

Theta took the doll, fingering the threadwork. "It looks like a sort of Apache voodoo doll with a stake through the heart. Not much of a joke."

Zane fluttered his fingers and spoke in a wavery voice. "It's a sign. The spirits are displeased." Dropping his hands, he turned to Clint. "Really, bro. We should just go home."

"Not going to happen, Zane. And if this is your way of scaring me into leaving, you should have put it on *my* pillow."

"Wasn't me, dude."

Theta served up coffee and breakfast burritos, tortillas stuffed with scrambled eggs, sausage, hash browns and cheese. Music on the tongue. I began to feel better.

As we ate, I heard the crunch and clop of new arrivals and looked up to see two horses approaching from the direction of the canyon's entrance. The riders dismounted and, at Darren's invitation, joined us for breakfast.

Both were young, mid-twenties maybe. The man was tall and thin, built like a pelican, with a jutting jawline and long, gangling legs. The woman was darkly pretty and slightly plump, her brown eyes flecked with gold. We made our introductions, and I learned the newcomers were Mike and Sarah Nichols.

"What brings you out here?" asked Theta.

Mike gave her a sardonic smile. "Looking for the mine," he admitted. "Aren't we all?"

We laughed and agreed, but I found myself wondering how close they'd camped to us last night, and how far they'd go to run off the competition or get their hands on Clint's map. It was easier to believe the pelican man had placed the menacing doll, than one of my companions. Might they have been trailing us?

Clint regarded the couple with curiosity, and a little suspicion. "Most folks come in on the northwest corner," he said. "What made you decide to head out this direction?"

"Geology," Mike answered. "I'm working on a masters in geological sciences at ASU."

"And I'm writing a thesis on native American cultures," Sarah added.

Mike nodded. "Both our interests have brought us into these mountains many times, and I've noticed that the geological makeup of the west side is not conducive to the formation of gold. But the eastern side is different. If there's gold in these mountains, I think it's bound to be east of LaBarge."

Clint's eyebrows rose on his forehead. "Interesting theory," he said. "You may have something there."

"Why aren't *you* looking on the west side?" Sarah challenged.

Clint shrugged. "It's been done to death. We're looking for a different angle."

"Fair enough," said Mike, grinning. He bowed to Theta. "My compliments to the chef, but we'd better be moving along. I wish you success in your search."

We murmured goodbyes, and I watched Mike and Sarah mount and direct their horses deeper into the canyon. I was relieved to see them go, and hoped we wouldn't run into them again. Not that I necessarily mistrusted them, but they were strangers and I was interested in keeping things simple.

As we finished packing up and clearing the camp site, the sky grew darker, like a falling shadow. I looked up through the tops of the canyon walls to see massed clouds, bruised purple and already dripping.

"Hold up," said Darren. "This will pass in a moment."

Theta's brow furrowed and she bit her lip. "If it doesn't," she warned, "we'd better head for high ground. Flash floods often sweep through these canyons after a heavy rain."

We huddled under the overhang and watched it pour for five minutes. Then, according to Darren's prediction, it blew off and the light filtering down into the gorge took on a golden hue. Mounting our horses, we started our procession through the canyon.

Mist rose from the sand as the sun's heat pulled the residue of rain from the ground, and the air smelt of freshened sagebrush. Sandia snorted, tossing her head, and Clint, riding in front of me, turned and smiled. He looked excited, his face almost as boyish as in those days long ago.

We didn't stop midday for lunch. "If we press on," Darren told us, "we can reach the next camp site by two o'clock. Then we can have a late lunch and relax."

When we reached the place, a bend in the canyon wall with another overhang, the last thing Clint wanted to do was relax.

"Eat up, fellas," he said to Zane and me. "After lunch, we're going exploring."

We ate, leaving Darren and Theta to establish our digs for the night while we set off on foot to see what lay beyond the bend. The ground was hardpan, pocked with sandy deposits and dotted with stubborn weeds. I paused to watch a black stink beetle lift its rear end in my direction, its shell as hard and shiny as a freshly waxed car.

We followed the curve of the stone walls as they twisted and turned, formed by some long forgotten river. We had no fear of getting lost. The gorge left but one way back and one way forward.

Until we reached the split.

Chapter 10

—·—

"Hello!" I shouted, listening for the echo and hearing only my own voice return—a weak, diminished version. Clint and Zane had gone together down one branch of the canyon, and I'd gone on my own down the other. For a while, we'd shouted at each other, sending crazy echoes bouncing along the stone corridor until they faded as we moved out of earshot.

I was alone.

The dry, mid-afternoon heat baked my skin and a trickle of sweat broke free from where my cowboy hat hugged my head, running down the side of my face. I swiped it away with my shirt sleeve and another sprang up in its place.

My footsteps sounded harsh and loud, grating the desert floor, the only noise discernible between those walls of stone. I moved deeper into the cleft of the canyon, glad of a little shadow as the sun moved farther to the west.

I trudged along for several minutes, gradually becoming aware of a sense of unease. Feeling certain I was hearing more than my own footsteps, I suddenly froze, listening for residual sounds. But there was nothing.

I'm not a fanciful man, but as the silence continued and shadows shifted, revealing here and there shallow caves and man-made indentations in the canyon wall, I sensed the presence of those long dead and I felt like a trespasser. Despite the sauna-like heat, I shivered, remembering the Apache doll on my pillow.

I shrugged the thought aside. Focusing my attention on the ancient stone, I tried to pick out landmarks that would have passed the test of time, hoping to find something recognizable from Jacob Waltz's map and instructions. He'd noted that at one point on the trail to the mine, the depressions in the canyon wall formed the semblance of a skull, with two eye sockets, and concavities for the nose and a scattering of teeth.

I watched for such an arrangement as I walked, sweeping my eyes along both sides of the gorge, but found nothing like it. The feeling that I was being followed grew stronger, and again I froze in my tracks and listened.

A faint pattering of footsteps filtered back to me, raising goosebumps along my spine. Something was in the canyon with me. Something not mortally human. I debated with myself whether I'd rather it be a ghost or some kind of animal.

I shook myself, licking my lips, tasting salt. It was surely something harmless. Continuing on, I rounded a gradual bend and stopped short when I saw the dead end.

A box canyon. The only way out was the way I had come in. I would be forced to encounter whatever was behind me.

Or would I?

As I cast my eyes about the stone wall, determined to finish my job of surveying for landmarks, I caught site of a series of chiseled indentations. Toeholds in a ladder to the top. I wondered if they'd been carved by some distant wanderer in a predicament similar to my own.

A wave of claustrophobia swept over me and suddenly an overwhelming desire to get up and out of the enclosing stone walls surged through me, setting up an urgent hum in my bloodstream. The distance to the top was maybe twenty-five feet, not a forbidding height, yet the thought of falling and lying helpless, vulnerable to any number of dangerous prospects, daunted me. I was not an experienced climber and I knew it needed a certain technique.

Trapped in the stone box, I stared back the way I had come, waiting, dreading. I imagined I heard the footfalls of an approaching unknown. At any moment, something might round that bend and be upon me.

Digging my hands into the carved-out niches, I pulled myself onto the stone ladder and climbed. The indentations were well-placed, a comfortable distance apart, until I reached the halfway point. I stopped. The next niche was out of my reach. Grabbing for it would require a drastic shift in balance. My throat hurt and I swallowed, but the painful lump persisted.

Again, I flashed back to the eucalyptus tree and how close I'd come to dying on that long-ago day. The earth beneath me was hard-packed and dotted with stones. I didn't want to fall.

Clinging to the rocky wall like an ant on a slender blade of grass, I feared climbing higher but the thought of backing my way down was equally unpleasant. As I considered my dilemma I heard a shuffling noise from above me and felt, rather than saw, a shadow.

A little shower of dust and minute pebbles rained down on me. Someone was up there.

Craning my neck, I peered up, the sun blinding me. I thought I glimpsed something—a face—on the lip of the cliff, but it vanished before I could be sure.

"Hello!" I shouted, my heart lifting, glad of some help or at least some encouragement. There was no answer.

Again, I called out but my appeal was met only by silence.

By now, the sweat was running profusely into my eyes, stinging and blurring my vision. The sun beat down, radiating off the bare rock, torrid enough to drive anyone mad. Maybe I was imagining the creature behind me, the presence above. Maybe it was all a desert mirage, driven by heat and superstition.

I lifted my head again, drawing breath for another shout, looking into the sky above me. And suddenly, the sun was blotted out, blocked by an object hovering at the edge of the cliff. A large stone.

As I watched, it wobbled once and then fell, plummeting toward me.

CHAPTER 11

— • —

THE STONE DROPPED WITH alarming speed, leaving me no time to think.

I sprang away from the rock wall, out of its path, and fell at the same frightening velocity.

We landed in the same moment, thudding to the sandy desert floor, sending up a whirl of dust. I tried to tuck and roll, but my position made it awkward and I landed on my left side, knocking the breath from my lungs. The ground, coarse and hot beneath my cheek, smelled strangely of the sea—heat, salt, and sand.

I lay with my eyes closed, allowing myself to drift in that beach dream, almost lulled into sleep and forgetting. The urge to give in, to give up, to avoid the pain of reality, held me in its powerful jaws and it took an awful wrench of will to drag my eyes open and deal with my situation.

My chest unclenched, and I pulled in a ragged breath, coughing a little, wincing at the pain. My left shoulder had borne the brunt of my fall. It ached, but I could rotate my arm and it seemed nothing was broken. My ribs would be woefully sore, and blood seeped from a bed of shallow abrasions on my face.

I'd managed to escape landing on rock and—more importantly—the rock hadn't landed on me. I looked up at the lip of the gorge, but if my assailant had peered down to see the result of his handiwork, he'd looked and left.

The skyline was empty.

Rising shakily to my feet, I stood bent over, hands braced on my knees, and let a wave of nausea pass. My canteen had survived the fall unscathed and I took a few swallows of tepid water, feeling better every moment. I stooped and retrieved my fallen hat, pulling it down over my sweaty hair.

What had been the reason for my attack? And who'd launched it? Either of the Halloways, knowing the territory, could have trailed me from above and heaved the rock over. Or the couple we'd met at breakfast.

Or someone entirely unknown.

At least it hadn't been a ghost. No vengeful spirit could have hefted the stone, at least two feet square and weighing fifty pounds or more.

I started back down the passage toward camp, worrying no longer about whatever had been following me before. Those faint, pattering footfalls paled into insignificance after my close call and I just wanted to get back to something familiar, a bit of shade, and a cold drink.

I hadn't gone twelve paces before I heard the muted echo of my name called. The voices grew stronger and a surge of relief left me almost too weak to walk. Clint and Zane were coming. I sagged against the canyon wall and let them come.

Clint's face paled as I explained what had happened, and then grew a mottled red with anger. He walked to the fallen rock and gazed up the toehold ladder to the rim above.

"I don't believe this," he said. "What does it mean?"

"It means we should go home, Clint." Zane, standing beside him, gave the rock a sullen kick.

"Or," I added, "it might mean we're getting uncomfortably close to finding the mine."

"What? You think someone's already found it and is keeping it a secret?" Zane asked.

"Why not?" I said. "I don't know much about gold mining, but it seems possible someone could be taking out small amounts of ore over time. Nothing to excite attention, but enough to discreetly supplement an income and set up for a nice retirement."

Clint shook his head. "I don't know how someone could get away with that."

"People get away with more than you might imagine, Bro," Zane said.

"So what do you want to do, Jay? I won't blame you if you want to pack it in. This is turning out to be more dangerous than I anticipated. Maybe we should call it quits."

I surprised myself by feeling a sinking disappointment. On the one hand, I wanted to return home, unharmed, and go back to the life I was used to. It was a good life, with comforts, challenges, rewards, and a family I loved.

On the other hand, Clint's desire for the thrill of the hunt had infected me and now that it seemed we might be close, I felt a strong tug pulling me forward. And to have my friend, my oldest friend, beside me as in our boyhood adventures...

"I say we ought to forge ahead," I said, and watched Clint's face light up.

"I'm so glad you feel that way, because we've got something exciting to show you. Are you sure you're okay?"

I moved all my parts and they seemed in functioning order, if a little sore. "Yes, I'm fine. What did you find?"

"Come on," he said. "We can get there and back before the sun dips too low."

He, Zane, and I retraced our steps and started down the other branch of the gorge. About half a mile along the passage Clint stopped and pointed up the canyon wall. The rock towered above us, much higher than the fork I'd explored earlier. As I stared, the shadows solidified, forming the skeletal face I'd been looking for.

"It's the skull landmark," I said.

"Right," Clint agreed. "And that," he said, gesturing toward a spire of stone, "could be the needle of rock on Jacob's map."

The three of us exchanged eager smiles and continued walking. But as we drew deeper into the gorge, the air seemed to thicken, resting heavy on my skin, pressing down with a dry, oppressive weight. It felt like being entombed with a mummified corpse and reminded me that death was no stranger in this desert land.

Niches decorated the sandstone walls of the canyon, some natural and others formed by primitive tools. I imagined unseen eyes peering at us from their darkened depths, hostile to our encroachment, and I was not the only one feeling a malevolent presence.

"This place is downright eerie," Clint said. "The mine must be guarded by spirits, like the genii around Aladdin's cave."

Zane laughed, and the sound reverberated in a hollow echo. "But you've got the open sesame, right bro?"

Clint stopped and pulled out his copy of the map. "Let's take a look."

He spread the paper against the rock face so we could get a good view of it. "We saw the skull and needle, and I think we passed this a while back," he said, indicating a towering rock depicted on the map.

"And that looks like the right grouping of cliff-dwellings," I remarked, pointing to a honeycomb of hollows in the wall.

"They all look the same after a while," Zane said. "You've seen one hole...you know the drill."

Clint refolded the map, a look of excitement settling into the curves of his face. He pointed toward another Y-shaped split ahead of us where the canyon branched apart.

"That's where we're headed come morning," he said. "Left branch. I think we're getting close."

CHAPTER 12

— · —

A FTER POLISHING OFF A plate of Theta's excellent garlic-laced spaghetti and meatballs, I sat back in my camp chair and fought my heavy eyelids to stay awake. The logs under the fire crackled and popped, sending up periodic showers of sparks and a drifting smoke that added to the hazy, dream-like atmosphere.

I hoped Clint wouldn't call on me to supply the evening's entertainment, and when Darren started in with some local folklore, I listened with gratitude and tired contentment, lacing my fingers over my full belly and gazing up at the stars.

"I can't let you folks go home," Darren started, "without hearing about Elisha M. Reavis, the crazy man of the mountain. Known as 'The Hermit,' Reavis was a college graduate from Illinois before he got bit by the gold bug and came out west. He failed in his efforts to find gold and tried to go back to what you might think of as a normal life. Became a teacher, got married, had a child."

Darren leaned forward and poked a stick into the fire. He pulled it out and watched smoke rise from the tip as he continued talking.

"The marriage broke up and he came back to Arizona, signed on as a U.S. Deputy Marshal. When that didn't work out either, he chucked it all and moved up into the mountains where he raised gardens and orchards and trained horses and mules for the military."

Darren never took his gaze off the charred end of his stick, waving it gently as if smoke-writing on the slate of darkness.

"Reavis earned his reputation as an eccentric. He grew a filthy, disgusting beard and never changed his pants. When one pair wore out, he'd just slap on another pair over the rags of the old. He never went anywhere without dragging along a train of mules, and he refused to enter any building where a woman was present."

The smoke trail from Darren's stick grew thin and he thrust it back into the coals, stirring up the scent of mesquite.

"One day," he continued, "Reavis caught an Indian brave skulking around on his property. He shot the man and left him where he lay. The next day, the brave's friend came looking for him and Reavis shot that man, too.

"Now he's got two dead natives on his land, just rotting in the southwestern sun. As you can imagine, the local tribe doesn't take kindly to this. So a few days later, a party of braves came and laid seige to Reavis's stronghold."

Pulling the stick from the fire, Darren once again waved it, watching it smoke. I'll admit I was mesmerized by it too, unable to tear my tired eyes away from the lazy circles of curling vapor.

"There was a gunfight. It lasted for hours. Round about sundown, Reavis ran out of ammunition and thought he was done for, but the Indians laid off shooting. It was their tradition not to fight after dark.

"So they set up a campfire, kind of like this one here," Darren said, returning the waning stick to the bed of embers. "They were just sitting around the fire, relaxing after a long hard day of shooting, when Reavis ran down into the midst of them. He was stark naked and wielding a butcher knife in each hand, screaming like a banshee and kicking up coals."

Darren leapt up and let out a blood-curdling scream that raised the hairs on the back of my neck. He waved the smoking stick in a frenzied figure-eight, its red tip flaring in the darkness. Zane sat opposite me and I saw flames dancing in his eyes as he followed the glowing progress of the stick with rapt attention.

"The natives freaked out because they thought he was a crazy man and their custom is never to kill a crazy man. If you do, they believed, you're destined to take his place and be as crazy as he is. So they ran off, and never bothered old Reavis again."

Darren blew on the end of his stick as if it was a smoking gun after a bullseye shot, and tossed it onto the fire. We applauded as he sank into his camp chair, a pleased grin spreading across his face.

"And on that triumphant note," Clint said, "I'm for bed."

We all echoed that thought and Theta poured a bucket of water on the dwindling coals, setting them hissing.

"Goodnight all," she said, but I thought her gaze lingered a fraction longer on Clint than on the rest of us. I scowled in his direction, and he had the grace to flush a little. Clearing his throat, he waved me a goodnight and turned toward his tent.

I started for mine, hoping my pillow would be free of Apache voodoo dolls. I thought about all the attendant dangers of the Arizona desert—scorpions, gila monsters, coiled snakes waiting to strike. And boulders that fall from above.

My heart pounded a bit faster as I remembered that moment, thrusting myself away from the canyon wall to avoid the hurtling stone, and I wondered if I'd be able to sleep.

Then I closed my eyes and slept like a rock.

CHAPTER 13

— • —

W E SET OUT AFTER breakfast the next morning. The day started off cooler than those that had gone before it, and the cliffs were tinged with blue and purple shadows, accentuated by the flutter and swoop of a flock of dark-winged birds.

The horses and mules clopped along the sandy trail, the sound of their hooves beating out a monotonous rhythm in my head. Clint's bay mare in front of me lifted her tail and dropped a mass of dung, scenting the delicate air of morning with the smell of horse-processed hay and oats.

An odd sensation rested in the pit of my stomach and I realized I wasn't looking forward to the day. That didn't make sense to me because everything pointed to a sensational day ahead, possibly culminating in the discovery of a gold mine people had searched after for more than a hundred years.

Clint was excited. I could see it in his posture, almost feel the buzz in the air around him. Zane rode behind me and when I turned to glance at him, his face puckered in a frown and he raised one shoulder in a shrug that said he was only along for the ride.

We reached the fork Clint had shown me the day before and branched to the left, trotting along in single file for more than an hour before the constricting walls drew apart and the canyon broadened slightly. We stopped.

"This is where you get off and go it on foot, boys," Theta said.

"Why?" I wondered out loud.

"You'll see," said Darren. "We'll stay here with the horses and wait for your triumphant return."

We dismounted and handed the reins over to the Halloways, arming ourselves with canteens and energy bars before forging ahead on foot.

"Be careful out there," Theta shouted after us, and I heard the note of worry in her voice. It resonated with my own concerns, but I pushed my doubts aside and hurried to catch up with Clint's excited strides.

The three of us continued along the rough-hewn stone wall and at length we rounded a bend and came to a stop where Darren's point became clear.

If a river ran along the bottom of the canyon, this portion of it would form a series of waterfalls. The only way to navigate down was by the use of rope ladders fastened at each fall, something a horse can't do.

Clint lowered himself onto the first rope ladder, testing it for stability.

"I don't know who put these here, but God bless 'em," he said. "This one feels sturdy enough."

He climbed down the eighteen-foot drop. Zane went next, and I followed, stopping at the bottom to remove my boot and toss out a stone that had somehow worked its way in. Clint had the map out, spread against the rock wall. He was nearly dancing with excitement.

"See this?" he said, pointing to an area near Jacob Waltz's symbol for the mine. "This series of drops looks like what Jacob drew here. I wondered why it looked like a staircase, but now it's clear." He licked his lips, eyes flashing with determination. Folding the map, he tucked it into his pocket and started for the next fall, some eighty yards distant, at a near run.

"Wait up," I shouted, jamming my foot back into my boot. Zane took off after him but fell behind, and Clint reached the dropoff alone. He didn't wait before starting down the ladder. The air felt light and clear and it seemed I could distinguish every crunch of gravel from Zane's boots as he followed his brother to the lip of the fall.

I heard, very distinctly, Clint's yelp of surprise as his head disappeared below the rim with the kind of suddenness that signals disaster. I ran forward, but Zane was well ahead of me and climbing down the ladder a good thirty seconds before me. By the time I reached the edge and looked down, there was already a pool of blood spreading out and soaking into the desert ground.

I scrambled down the rope ladder, scarcely noticing the broken rung that dangled uselessly in splintered tatters as I rushed to my best friend's side like he had to mine so many years ago.

"Clint!" I shouted, bending over him. "Clint, stay with me."

His eyes stared into mine, the pupils huge, swallowing up the dark blue irises. He opened his mouth to speak, but only a puff of air escaped.

I grabbed his hand, rubbing it, willing him to live.

"Clint, don't you dare leave me. This was your idea and you're damn well going to see it through!"

I knelt over him, shouting, bullying him to stay with me until help came.

But he didn't.

CHAPTER 14

— · —

S HOCK WASHED OVER ME in waves and I felt dizzy as the black shadows of swooping birds flickered across the canyon floor. Shuddering, I shifted my eyes away from the pooling blood of my best friend.

This couldn't be real. I took a step back, casting around desperately, certain I could find a way to rewind this and play it back differently if I only looked hard enough. I turned my gaze to the ground beneath Clint's head, searching for the stone that had done this, but only dirt and tiny pebbles showed, glistening crimson in the desert sun.

"How can this be?" I asked Zane. My head felt light, as if it would lift off my shoulders and float away. I realized I was shaking and dropped to a sitting position, putting my head between my knees and working to breathe.

When I felt control returning, I crawled to Clint's body. I had to know. For some reason, I felt compelled to see the instrument of his death. I lifted his head as gently as I could but detected no wound there. Instead, I realized the blood came from lower down. I turned him slightly and experienced another wave of shocked unreality.

A jagged shaft of red stone.

I dropped my friend's shoulder and scuttled away, pushing my back against the sun-blazed slab of stone behind me, trying to make sense of what I saw. I stared up the side of the canyon to where a maze of cliff-dwellings honeycombed the stone wall, the sense of hostile eyes on me stronger than ever.

The air seemed to shimmer with ghostly whisperings. Something rose in my throat and I swallowed in revulsion, thinking of the thing protruding from Cliff's back.

My friend had been stabbed to death by a chiseled spike of stone, and no living being had been within thirty feet of him when it happened.

CHAPTER 15

A TERRIBLE SILENCE SEEMED to expand within the gorge, pressing against me, making it hard to breathe. No whispering wind or rattling insect made a noise. No echo of shrieking bird or yipping coyote. I felt as if I tried to speak, the words would fall into a vacuum and hurtle through eternity, unheard by human ears. The sensation was eerie beyond description.

Zane, too, appeared to be in shock. Our reluctance to accept that Clint was gone isolated us from one another, creating an emotional distance neither one of us wanted to cross at that moment. To look each other in the eye, to truly connect, would mean facing the truth, and neither of us was ready.

Finally, I felt able to speak. "Stay with your brother," I said. "I'll go for help."

My legs were numb as I retraced our steps but once I started moving, a dreadful sort of desperation fell over me and my pace quickened until I ran like the bats of hell dogged my heels. I stumbled on loose stones and petrified branches, falling once and catching myself with the palms of my hands on the desert scree. Ignoring the sting of a dozen scrapes, I hefted myself up and hurried on.

By the time I neared camp, my shirt was soaked with sweat and my heart was pounding like a jackhammer in my chest. I stopped and crouched down, dry retching over a patch of weeds. Ahead I heard a shout and the sound of running feet. Darren reached me first, but it was Theta's worried voice I heard.

"What's wrong?" she demanded. "Where's Clint?"

Somehow, I made them understand what had happened. That Clint had been stabbed, that he was dead. I watched Darren's lips press together and flatten, his eyebrows drawing down into a dark vee above his nose. Theta started to cry.

Darren saddled a horse, shoving bottles of water and provisions into the saddlebags.

"It'll be mid-afternoon by the time I get where I can raise a signal on the radio. Sit tight, and I'll be back with help as soon as I can."

He kissed Theta and gave me a grim nod before swinging himself up and departing at a fast trot.

I sank into a camp chair, letting my arms droop over the sides, and thought about the Bible verse that talks about lifting the hands that hang down, strengthening the feeble knees. I thought it was somewhere in the New Testament. Clint would know.

It hit me then, with a fresh wave of shock and grief. Clint might know, but I couldn't turn to him and ask.

Never again.

At least, not on this side of the Great Divide. The upheaval in my gut told me I had some troubled times ahead in the struggle to accept that Clint was gone. That I hadn't been able to save him like he'd saved me.

I had failed.

Theta knelt beside me, her eyes rimmed with red, a sprinkling of freckles standing out against her pale and lovely face.

"Will you stay with the horses? I'm going to be with Zane," she said. "And with Clint."

Her voice caught, and she stopped, pulling back and shaking her head, sending a swirl of chestnut hair across her face like a privacy curtain. Without another word, she walked away and I watched until she rounded a bend in the gorge and disappeared.

I was alone.

CHAPTER 16

—·—

THE POLICE CAME, ARRIVING on horseback with the dawn.

The sound of plodding hooves woke me and a chill in the air seemed to settle over my heart, bringing out a rash of goosebumps on my arms. The raw morning was filled with a bleakness that made it hard for me to stir from the sleeping bag I'd finally crawled into last night. But I knew the police would want to speak to all of us as soon as possible.

I dragged on a pair of jeans. They felt clammy against my skin and my fingers fumbled with the zipper, numb and clumsy. There was a murmur of voices as I left my tent, Theta Halloway greeting the new arrivals in somber tones. Darren was absent.

When he'd returned from summoning the police, he'd taken a shotgun and sent Zane and Theta back from their vigil over Clint's body. He'd been there all night, keeping away predators, securing the area.

That familiar odor that always smelled to me like a screen door hung heavy in the air and I wondered if it might rain again. The sky above the canyon walls shone with a dusting of pale blue streaked with pink, and the chatter of birds was just beginning.

I felt tired beyond words.

As I walked toward the campfire, I noticed the police had brought more than horses on the journey. An all-terrain vehicle that looked like it belonged on the moon lumbered along behind them on triangular tracked wheels. It pitched and righted itself on the uneven surface of the desert like an alien beast, adding to my feeling that none of this was real.

"Good morning, sir," said the man in charge as I approached. "I'm Chief Deputy Madsen, and this is my partner, Deputy Steele. Officers Crawley and Whittaker," he nodded toward the moon rover, "are crime scene specialists."

He held out a hand and I shook it. "I'm sorry for your loss," he said, sounding sincere. After a respectful pause, he added, "Can I get your name, sir?"

I introduced myself, and Deputy Steele took note. Both were dressed in khaki sheriff's uniforms, but not the buttoned-down kind you'd put on for office work. More like battle gear. Their expressions were solemn, and it struck me they were serious professionals, on the job.

And in this case, their job involved the murder of my best friend.

The ATV rolled past and kept on going, heading off to where Clint waited for them.

Zane joined us and shook hands with the deputies as Theta brought a coffee pot and a stack of styrofoam cups. We each held a cup as she poured the steaming brew, fragrant vapor rising in the cold morning air. As Zane sat in a camp chair and lifted the cup to his lips, I saw Madsen nod to Steele.

"If you don't mind, Mr. Fuller," Steele said to Zane, "I'd like you to go through what happened."

Zane started to speak, but Steele held up a hand. "Let's take our chairs over there," he said, gesturing to a grouping of rocks several yards distant.

Zane paused, and I saw his jaw tighten. "Okay."

He stood and picked up the chair, avoiding my gaze. The two of them moved off and Madsen turned to me, pulling a small notepad from his pocket.

"Will you tell me how it happened, Mr. Bohmer?"

It began sinking in that if Clint had been murdered, we were all suspects. When I'd woken from the sweet forgetting of sleep, and the awful memory of Clint's demise had flooded back, it seemed nothing worse could happen.

But the day had just grown a shade darker.

I told what had happened, including as much detail as I could remember. Madsen's shrewd eyes watched my face as I answered and I'd seen enough television to know he was gauging my responses, watching my body language. I hoped I passed muster.

He made note of everything I said and asked questions to clarify.

"What time was it when you left the camp?"

"I haven't been paying much attention to time since we left civilization. It doesn't seem to matter as much out here, so I can't say for sure. I think it must have been sometime between eight and nine o'clock."

"And how long would you say it took you on foot to reach the rope ladders?"

"I'd guess maybe forty-five minutes."

"And you say your friend was killed on the second of the rope ladders?"

"Yes. He ran ahead and went down alone."

"Who reached him first?"

"His brother, Zane. I had a rock in my boot and stopped to get it out, so I'd fallen behind."

"How long did it take you to catch up and see what had happened?"

I thought about it, remembering that moment when Clint's head had suddenly dropped from view, the sound of his cry as he fell.

"I shoved my boot on and ran. It's hard to judge how long it took."

"Give me your best guess."

"Must have been about thirty seconds or so."

He wrote it down, then met my eye. "A lot can happen in thirty-odd seconds."

"You're telling me. I lost my best friend."

"I am sorry, Mr. Bohmer." He paused. "Take a moment to think back. Do you remember seeing anything odd? Did you hear anything, or notice anything, to indicate someone else might be present?"

I remembered that skin-crawling feeling I'd had, looking at the small network of depressions in the canyon wall.

"There *was* something," Madsen said. "I see the memory in your face."

"It was only a feeling. Like being watched. The place was pretty barren except for a patch of cave dwellings. But there wouldn't have been time for someone to attack Clint and disappear into those caves without being seen."

"Is there anywhere else someone could have been hiding?"

I thought back, but all I remembered was an impression of emptiness and the eerie feeling of eyes watching.

"I don't know."

"Okay," Madsen said, making a note. "Describe what happened after you arrived."

"I climbed down the ladder...I remember now, one of the rungs was broken, just hanging, barely attached to the rest of the ladder. That must have been what broke and made him fall. When I climbed down, Clint was still alive. He looked at me but he couldn't speak—"

My voice broke, and I stopped, swallowing hard, working to get control.

A minute passed. Then I said, "I tried to get him to stay with me, to wait for help."

Gulping down a wavering breath, I skipped past the moment when I felt Clint leave me and moved to what happened after that, when everything had changed.

"I thought he'd hit his head on rock, but he hadn't." I paused, not sure how to say what I wanted to convey. "It looked like he'd been shot."

Madsen's eyes widened slightly and his gaze sharpened. "Darren led me to understand your friend was stabbed."

"I said it *looked* like he'd been shot. I mean, like the doll."

The deputy's hand poised above the notepad. "The doll?"

I felt my face grow hot. "A couple nights ago, someone left a sort of voodoo doll on my pillow. It was made to look as if it had been shot in the back with a stone arrow. Like Clint."

Madsen clicked his ballpoint, putting pad and pen back in his pocket.

"I want to see this doll," he said. "Now."

Chapter 17

— • —

A FTER I'D SHOWN CHIEF Madsen the doll and answered
more questions, I took a nap. I zipped my tent closed and
curled on my sleeping bag, letting the heat cover me in sweat,
feeling it bake my bones. Drifting off, I was able to forget, to lift
the burden of reality and float in a world of dreams.

When I woke, the sun had sunk below the canyon walls
and purple shadows muted the stark landscape. The mantle of
remembering settled once more on my shoulders, heavy with
regret. I realized my work now would be in moving past this
point, slowly shedding the grief until only the sweetness of
eternal friendship remained.

Learning the truth about what had happened to Clint would
be an essential part of that healing.

Emerging from my tent, I saw the police had set up a small
camp of their own about fifty yards further along the canyon
wall. I set off toward it, intending to ask Chief Madsen for an
update. But as I approached, I heard voices from within the tent

and froze. If they were discussing the case, I wanted to hear their unfiltered speculations.

Stepping carefully, silently on the cracked and dusty desert floor, I moved closer, making sure my shadow wouldn't fall across the canvas, alerting them to my presence. My mother had years ago taught me it was wrong to eavesdrop, but I felt no shame. Only a driving desire to find out what had happened to my friend.

And why.

Straining my ears, I heard snippets of a conversation between Madsen and his partner, Steele.

"...lied about it," Steele was saying. "I did some digging and found out neither one of them is registered at Arizona State."

A little thrill of shock went through me as I realized he must be talking about the couple who'd stopped by to share our breakfast on that first morning. Mike and Sarah Nichols, I recalled. He'd claimed to be working on some sort of geology degree and she was studying Native American cultures. Taking a step closer to the tent, I closed my eyes and focused on listening.

"...he violated the restraining order and was arrested." Steele's voice again.

"Let me guess," Madsen said, "the case never went to trial."

"Right. Judge threw it out. Petty theft and precious little evidence. But it seems clear that the Nichols operate by stalking searchers for the lost mine, hoping to poach their findings."

"And they stoop to stealing whatever they can when the treasure doesn't turn up."

"Which is inevitable," Steele said, "because no one will ever find it."

I heard a snort, Madsen rendering his opinion. "What did you find out about the Halloways?" he asked.

"Nothing more than what everybody around here already knows. Her first husband was murdered—"

"And they were both suspects," Madsen finished. "Sure. But they were both cleared, and frankly, I never bought into the theory that Theta murdered her husband."

"I know, Chief," Steele said. "But what about Darren?"

"Hush," Madsen warned.

I took that as my cue to back off. I'd heard enough to keep the wheels in my head spinning for a good long while and I didn't want to get caught crouching outside the police tent. I needed some time to process all the bits and pieces whirling around my brain.

I walked, randomly choosing my path, and found myself back in the box canyon where I'd nearly been smashed by a falling rock just two days earlier. It felt like a lifetime ago. A dry, dusty lifetime, without Clint and his crazy schemes to brighten it.

Who had pushed that rock over the edge? Was it the same person who'd killed my best friend?

This time, as I trudged through the constricting passage, I heard nothing in pursuit, nothing above me on the ridge.

Nothing.

When I reached the dead end, I sank onto the scratchy sand, shaded by the wall of the gorge. I stared down the hazy stone corridor and let my mind go blank, washed clean as desert granite after a storm.

I don't know how long I sat like that, empty and still. The shadows had deepened around me, their gloom almost tangible, like cobwebs I must push through to return to the land of human habitation. I rose and began the trek back, listening to the rhythmic crunch of my boots on grit and rock, echoing faintly in the narrow channel.

CHAPTER 18

— · —

I WAS BACK IN time for dinner. Falling into a camp chair by the fire, I picked at the plate Theta put in my lap. The two sheriff's deputies were eating with us, but I saw no sign of the ATV or its occupants.

"What happens now?" I asked.

Madsen used a piece of bread to sop the last of the beans and sauce from his plate, popping it into his mouth and chewing before he answered. "The specialists have finished with the crime scene and are on their way to the medical examiner's office with the body. The rest of us will be here for another day or two."

Zane tossed a paper cup onto the fire. "What for?" he asked.

I watched the cup blacken and burn as it caught the flames.

"I want to spend some time checking out the scene myself," Madsen said, "and I want you all on hand in case I have any questions you can answer."

And because we're all suspects.

"Darren tells me you folks encountered another couple up here," he continued. "The Nichols. I want to locate them and see if they have anything to add to the investigation."

I wished I could be around to see how that interview panned out, but doubted I'd have the opportunity of another eavesdrop session. I tried to relax the tension from my shoulders. I told myself to be patient, that the officials would identify Clint's killer and answer the questions that burned through my body and soul.

Despite the nap, I was tired enough to crawl back into my tent by 9:30. I lay staring into the shadows gathered in the olive green recesses, letting thoughts and images circle around my brain without grabbing hard onto any one of them for a closer look.

As the campfire outside dwindled down to coals, the shadows thickened. Night dropped its blanket over me and I slept.

The first moments after I woke felt like any other day, making the memory land like a punch to the gut when it came. The morning light was cold and colorless, grating harsh against my eyes as I pulled on my jeans. The fabric felt stiff against my skin, and grubby.

The romantic charm of this trip had long since worn off.

Darren had a fire going and I saw Madsen discreetly heading for a bush. Theta handed me a cup of coffee as I came to stand beside her.

"How's Zane doing," I asked her.

"I haven't seen him and he's not in his tent. I'm guessing he needed some solitude to process his grief."

What she said made sense, but a chill of foreboding crept over me. I swallowed the last of my coffee and grabbed my hat and canteen. I found Darren feeding the horses.

"I'm going to see if I can find Zane," I told him, keeping my voice low.

He nodded, and I set off in the same direction we'd gone last time we were together, the three of us—me, Zane, and Clint. The morning was still and silent, no swooping birds, no cooing doves. Only the sound of my boots scuffing along on the desert floor.

As I walked, the sun rose high enough to peep over the edge of the canyon wall, spilling a wash of pale lemon yellow into the gray of the day. The faint scent of warming sage and mesquite followed me as I made my way to the giant staircase and started down the first ladder.

As I neared the place of Clint's demise, the weight in my chest grew heavier. I had a fatalistic feeling I knew where Zane had gone.

And I was right.

I found him in the same place I'd last seen Clint. At the bottom of a broken ladder, lying in a pool of blood.

CHAPTER 19

— · —

Z ANE HAD BEEN LUCKIER than his brother.

The stone spike had missed his heart, catching him nearer the shoulder, narrowly missing the tip of his lung. He'd lain there on the cold desert floor for hours before I went searching, and might have died from shock.

But he hadn't.

The crime scene specialists returned with their outlandish vehicle. While the police worked to process the area and transport Zane to the hospital in Florence, I helped the Halloways strike camp and load the horses and mules. Plans had changed, and Madsen ordered us back to the ranch.

The outward trek seemed to take ages longer than going in had done. Breaking our journey once again at the naturally formed ramada, Darren made a fire for warmth and cooking, but there was no music, no stories, no laughter. The three of us sat glum and silent after our evening meal, staring into the sputtering flames, listening to them crackle.

I couldn't believe Clint was gone.

By evening of the following day, we'd reached the gate of the Halloway property. I was more exhausted than I ever remembered being, physically and emotionally wrung out. I felt like I should visit Zane at the hospital, but I just couldn't face it.

I called my wife instead, and felt an ache in my gut so sharp I almost gasped from the pain of it. I wanted her with me. I needed to feel her cool hand smooth over my brow, her soft lips, kissing, consoling. Helping me forget.

We spoke for twenty minutes and I made do with the sound of her voice.

And then, as the last orange rays fell beneath the horizon and the world went dark, I drank a beer and went to bed.

CHAPTER 20

—·—

T HE NEXT MORNING, I drove to the hospital. It had rained in the night and muddy puddles flanked the road, sending up sprays of dirty water and leaving a dismal film on the windshield of my rental. The parking lot was full and I circled four times before finding a cramped spot to pull into.

Zane was sleeping when I arrived, but Detective Madsen met me in the waiting room and waved me into a chair upholstered with something like vinyl. It squeaked as I sank down, as if I'd disturbed a family of mice nesting in the cushion.

"Do you have any idea who did this?" I asked, trying not to think about the whisper-like sounds echoing in the canyon after I discovered the spike in Clint's back.

Madsen regarded me with a penetrating gaze. I felt exposed, as if he could read my thoughts like a marquis on my forehead. After a long moment, he said, "We searched the cliff dwellings in range of the place where your friend died."

I said nothing. He raised an eyebrow and continued. "This is not something we want the press to get hold of, so I'm trusting your discretion, Mr. Bohmer."

"I understand," I said, bracing myself, wondering how bad it could be after the worst had already happened.

"We found a crossbow," he said. "Stashed in a clump of chaparral."

I stared. "What are you saying? Someone shot Clint with a stone arrow from a crossbow? Is that even possible?"

Madsen held my gaze. "I wouldn't have thought so," he replied.

I felt stunned. Who? Why?

Madsen saw fit to impart another piece of information. "The bow has been modified. We're running tests now to see if the stone dagger that killed Clint could have been fired from the weapon."

A hint of a smile curved his lips. "I have to admit, my ballistics experts are finding it an interesting challenge."

"A real switch from business as usual, I guess."

"One for the text books," he agreed.

There was something I wanted to ask him, but I was afraid of how he might take it. How it would make me sound.

"Is the bow a modern one?" I asked at last. "Or...primitive?"

He looked at me with a strange expression. "Modern," he replied. "Whatever your superstitions, I assure you a living, breathing person perpetrated these crimes."

I didn't consider myself a superstitious person, but I didn't bother trying to explain. I didn't think I could put voice to the thoughts and worries scurrying around in my brain.

"So that's what we're looking at?" I asked. "Someone hid in the cliffs and shot Clint—and later Zane—with a stone projectile from a crossbow?"

"I didn't say that." Madsen cleared his throat. "But we have to consider the possibility."

After he left, I bought a candy bar from a vending machine and went back to see if Zane was awake.

"That looks good," he said. "Better than what they're serving."

I put the candy on the tray in front of him and he picked it up, peeling off the wrapper. He chewed and neither one of us said anything for a while.

Finally, I swallowed the lump in my throat and said, "I'm so sorry Clint is gone. The world is a poorer place today." Bunching my fists, I stuffed them into my jacket pockets. "I will always miss him."

Zane bowed his head and seemed to be fighting tears. He put the half-eaten candy bar on the bedside tray and pushed it away. His right hand was bandaged, and for something to say, I asked him what happened to it.

"Picked up a splinter from that damn rope ladder. Got infected. I'm on antibiotics now, along with everything else."

At least you're alive.

We talked for a while, neither one of us mentioning Clint, then I left and went to the hospital chapel.

I took a seat in the third pew and waited. Sunlight filtering through the stained glass window fell in jewel-toned shapes across the tile floor, bringing a glowing warmth into the quiet space.

There were voices here, too. Whisperings from the dead and grieving, but they comforted me and I let them flow. I thought about my best friend, how I hadn't been able to save him like he had me, and that failing hurt me like a spike through my own chest.

I thought of Clint sprawling there on the desert floor, his lifeblood spilling out onto the thirsty earth. I thought of the spike in his heart, a giant splinter of killing stone.

A splinter.

And I saw it.

Incredibly, I knew what happened, how it happened, and who had done it.

I caught Detective Madsen before he left the hospital.

CHAPTER 21

— · —

"Z ANE KILLED CLINT," I told Madsen.

We stood outside the gift shop where I'd stopped him on his way out. Vases and bright bouquets of flowers decked the window, their fragrance floating lightly on the air. A woman brushed past us, carrying a bunch of helium-filled balloons toward the bank of elevators.

"And I have some ideas about how to prove it," I continued.

Madsen's face showed a peculiar mix of annoyance and amusement. "Let's find a quiet corner to talk."

We settled into a pair of chairs in a deserted hallway. I twisted sideways, facing him head on, eager to convey my ideas and win his support.

"Zane claims he injured his hand by picking up a splinter from the broken rung of the ladder. If we had the splinter they extracted from his infected finger, it might go a long way toward convincing a jury he had something to do with Clint's death."

"How do you figure?"

"I climbed down that ladder right after Zane did. The broken rung dangled off to the side. It was almost detached, hanging by a few fibers of rope. There was no reason to touch the rung itself while climbing down. I didn't."

Madsen raised his eyebrows and motioned me to go on.

"I think that splinter could help us wangle a confession in one of two ways. I believe Zane either got the splinter when he tampered with the rung, knowing Clint would be the first one to use the ladder in his characteristic rush to find the mine."

Madsen tipped his head. "Or?"

"Or, it wasn't a wooden splinter at all that caused the infection. It was a splinter of stone."

A hint of a smile touched Madsen's lips. "I had a similar thought," he said. "That's why I had the nurse save the offending splinter. We're just waiting now, for the lab analysis." He paused. "What made you think of it?"

"No one was anywhere near Clint when he fell from that ladder. Zane got to him first, and had as much as thirty seconds before I arrived to look down. He was the only one with opportunity, so it had to be him. I just didn't know how, or why."

"And you do now?"

I winced. "I see it in my mind, over and over like a nightmare, how it must have happened. The only way it could have happened."

Bracing myself, I went on. "Here's how I picture it. The night before, while we were sleeping, Zane tampered with the rung so that it would break under Clint's weight. Then he waited for Clint to run ahead, and made sure he was right behind him. The sabotaged rung was close to the top of the ladder, ensuring that I'd hear and see Clint when he cried out and fell."

My stomach did a queasy flip-flop in my gut as I played the scene out in my mind, a nightmare that would likely stay with me for life. I clenched my fists and pressed on.

"Zane ran to help, and when he reached his brother, winded and flat out on his back on the canyon floor, Zane raised Clint's left shoulder, placed the spike beneath, and used his boot to stomp down on Clint's chest, driving the spike up into his heart."

Madsen met my gaze with a steady eye. "Then who stabbed Zane?" he challenged.

"He did."

The eyebrows rose a bit higher, but he said nothing.

"To remove suspicion from himself and throw confusion on motives," I continued. "He went to the same place, with the same sort of spike—clearly carved out of stone beforehand—and laid down on it, driving it into his shoulder. That's why it wasn't in as deep."

Madsen grimaced. "That's a lot of pain and risk to bring on oneself."

I nodded. "He must have thought it worth the risk. As for the pain, the paramedics gave him morphine when they arrived, but I'll bet a blood test would have shown he was already medicated. I doubt Zane would have caused such a painful injury to himself without pharmaceutical assistance."

Madsen leaned back in his chair and seemed to be studying the eye chart on the pale green wall opposite where we sat. "I'm following your logic, but it's all a bit far-fetched. Why would Zane do this?"

I rose from the chair and straightened my shoulders, not willing to back down. Once I'd seen the truth and accepted it in all its awful glory, I needed to justify my conviction that Zane had killed his own brother. My best friend.

I needed to know why.

"Let's ask him," I said.

CHAPTER 22

— • —

"I'M GOING TO TALK to our suspect," Madsen said, his eyes stony, his tone grim. "There's only one way you're going in with me—and that's with your mouth shut."

Gripping me by the forearm, he said, "Is that clear?"

I was itching to ask Zane my questions, to demand his answers, but I didn't want to lose this tenuous foothold I had into the investigation. Biting back my disappointment, I nodded. "Yes, sir."

"Until we have something more conclusive than hunches and splinters, I'm asking you to keep your suspicions to yourself and let me do the talking. You are here in your capacity as a family friend, and only that."

"Okay," I agreed.

The corridor smelled strongly of pine cleaner as we approached Zane's room. A janitor swabbed the floor at the far end of the hallway, a yellow slip hazard placard marking off the spot. We turned into room 224 and I saw Zane's dark head drooping against the whiteness of the pillow. He straightened as we entered, rubbing a hand across his forehead in a weary gesture that managed to convey a subtle annoyance.

"Sorry to disturb you again, Mr. Fuller," Madsen began, "but I need to ask you a few more questions."

Zane folded his hands, resting them on his sheet-covered belly, and waited.

"Your brother was a very wealthy man," Madsen said. "Do you know if he left a will?"

Zane rolled his eyes. "My brother was, as you say, a wealthy man. Of course he left a will." He paused. "At least, I assume he did."

"But you don't know for sure?"

"We discussed it once. Years ago. So I know he made a will at some point."

"Did you discuss the terms of the will? Did he tell you who stood to inherit in the event of his death?"

Zane's eyes widened. "Well, I do, of course. In large part, anyway. We only had each other. Our parents were killed in a boating accident over a decade ago."

A small silence fell over the room. Zane's eyes narrowed.

"With your resources," he said, "you ought to be able to figure out who his attorney was and get your hands on a copy of the document."

Madsen gave a dry cough. "Indeed. And that we have, Mr. Fuller." His hand went to his breast pocket, tapping the folded paper resting there. "You may be interested to know the actual terms of your brother's will. While he left you a modest monthly stipend, the bulk of his estate goes to his friend, Mr. Jay Bohmer."

I felt my knees buckle and my mouth go dry. I had not seen this coming, always believing it would be the other way around. Two spots of high color had risen on Zane's cheeks. His lips trembled.

"That can't be right," he said. "I'm sure you're mistaken."

Madsen regarded him silently, saying nothing.

A deep groan, starting as a low rumble and crescendoing into a full-volume shriek tore from Zane's chest.

"You're wrong! You're wrong! You...are...wrong."

Breathing heavily, Zane stared at us, eyes hard as marbles in his florid face. A nurse bustled into the room, glaring disapprovingly as she checked her patient's vital measurements.

"I must ask you to leave," she said. "You'll have to come back later."

"Yes," Madsen agreed. "We're finished here." He locked eyes with Zane. "For now."

We left the room and Madsen went directly to the nurse's station where he borrowed the phone.

"I'm putting a man on watch," he told me, indicating the chair outside room 224. "On duty 24/7."

He gave me a weak smile. "Go back to the ranch and get some rest. Don't wander. As Clint Fuller's main heir, you still have the biggest motive for wanting him dead."

Stunned, I opened my mouth to protest, but he waved me silent. "Easy, Mr. Bohmer. I'm not accusing you just yet, but I want to know where I can find you. Stay close."

We met eyes and shook hands. Working to steady my breathing, I walked away down the corridor, my footsteps echoing in the sterile, pale green canyon.

CHAPTER 23

THE HIGH DESERT SUN had soaked up the puddles by the time I drove back to the ranch, leaving dried mud and silt in patches on the road. Pulling into the parking lot, I climbed out of my rental and headed for the lobby, my steps in rhythm with the mournful cooing of the doves.

Theta Halloway let me have the key to Clint's room. I wanted to sit among his things, smell his presence, ask his advice about what I should do. I needed time to think.

Letting myself in, I felt an immediate emptiness that dragged at the corners of my heart. But as I ran my hands over the comb and aftershave he'd left on the granite slabbed bathroom counter and saw the jumble of shoes and clothing scattered on the unmade bed, I began to feel a slight lift in my chest.

Clint was gone. But he had been here. Alive on the planet. And he'd left his impression in many ways and on many people. He'd made a difference.

I walked to the glass cube that formed the atrium at the center of the room. I clicked open the lock and slid the door wide. It glided smoothly along its track with a muted hiss and I stepped into the sunlit space. It felt strange, the contrast between the air-conditioned coolness of the room and the heat of the open air.

As I let the warring currents play over me, the cell phone in my pocket buzzed and I pulled it free. Glancing at the screen, I saw a message from Detective Madsen:

Lab results in, stone test positive

I supposed that meant the lab technicians had identified the splinter taken from Zane's finger as coming from the stone murder weapon, rather than the broken rung as he'd claimed. The bits of evidence were stacking up, but Madsen had a ways to go before he could present a solid case.

Hearing a noise, I caught a blur of motion from the corner of my eye. I turned and saw Zane standing on the other side of the glass, looking in at me, his face twisted into a mask of chilling malice. He held a shopping bag in one hand, pulled taut with the weight of something inside.

I took a step toward the atrium's opening, but he blocked my way, standing with knees slightly bent, his jaw locked and a hard look in his eye. Twinges of alarm fired in my gut.

"Zane! What are you doing here? You need to be in the hospital."

I wondered how he'd gotten past Madsen's guard, but pushed the worry aside. In this moment, it just didn't matter.

"Wrong, Jay," he said, his voice high and eerily sing-song. "This is the only place I need to be right now. This is all I need to do."

His tone, his expression, the fury radiating off him in waves told me I was in trouble. I had a sudden flash of memory—flames dancing in Zane's eyes as he listened to Darren's story about the crazy man of the mountain, staring mesmerized at the glowing stick in Darren's hand.

It gave me an idea.

A wild idea, with only a fraction of a chance of succeeding. But if Elisha M. Reavis's ruse of running screaming and naked into a mess of American Indians had worked, mine just might too.

"No, Zane," I told him, putting compassion in my voice and a look of concern on my face. "You really need to be in the hospital. You're dangerously ill. We—"

I broke off and shrugged. Zane narrowed his eyes, suspicious.

"What are you talking about?"

I hesitated as long as I dared, but I needed to keep his attention focused where I pointed it. "We didn't want to tell you until the lab results came in—"

"Tell me what? What lab results?"

I frowned. "The stone that stabbed you was contaminated by an organism, some kind of bacterial agent, that's causing your cells to mutate rapidly. The doctors don't know how to stop it. That antibiotic they gave you was meant to counteract the process, but..."

I took a step closer and held my cell phone up so he could see the screen with Madsen's message. He snatched it from me, scowling as he read.

"The doctors are trying everything," I continued, "consulting experts all over the world, but Zane...you should prepare yourself. They predict you have only hours to live."

He hurled the phone at my feet and I felt a surge of gratitude toward my wife, who'd made sure I covered the screen with tempered glass.

"You're a lying sack of garbage, Jay. I never understood why my brother valued you so highly." His voice was a vindictive sneer as he added, "Above his own kin, apparently."

He stood braced across the atrium door and I knew I wasn't getting out of there until he'd vented his rage. Stooping, I retrieved my phone and surreptitiously activated an audio recording app I sometimes used during interviews with clients while I continued to deliver the bad news to Zane.

Knowing it could get me killed.

"The stone through Clint's heart harbored the same organism. He would have shared your same fate," I said, "but he was lucky enough to die fast, before the bacteria had time to attack his blood."

I lifted my shoulders in a gesture of helplessness. "Yours will be an agonizing death, I'm afraid. But the doctors can help manage your pain. You need to go back, Zane."

He stared at me, not wanting to believe. But as I watched, a parade of expressions crossed over his features—incredulity, fear, and finally, acceptance.

Followed by white hot anger.

"The Apache curse of the damned," he said, grinding the words out with a guttural growl. "That's what this is. Jacob Waltz's deal with the dead."

He choked out a laugh, soft at first but growing in a maniacal crescendo. It shot a chill down my spine, even as I stood in that glass shaft of desert heat.

"The old Apaches put a stop to Clint's charmed life in the end, didn't they, Jay? He always got the best of everyone, reaped the richest rewards, had the greatest luck. While I settled for what was left."

Zane's eyes were bright with fever, a result of his infection, and I knew its sole cause was not the tainted splinter, but a tainted soul.

"I worked in a welding shop, Jay. For twenty years. Do you have any idea how grueling a life that is? How damaging and demeaning? While my brother sailed his yachts and flew his jets.

He sat behind a desk and produced millions of dollars with the wave of a finger while I..."

Zane uttered a frenzied roar, baring his teeth like a maddened animal.

"And then—here's the part that really burned me up, Jay—he tried to throw it all away on seeking for more treasure."

I watched Zane's nostrils flare, going white against the red of his suffused face. "Oh no," he screamed. "Not while he still had an inheritance to pass on to me. He had to be stopped."

I drew a deep breath. "Are you confessing to Clint's murder?" I asked.

He gave me a baleful glare. "Yes. Why not? I'll be dead myself by tomorrow, so it was all for nothing. But you," he said. "I can't leave you to scoop up all that should have been mine."

Raising his chin, he glowered at me as he plunged his hand into the shopping bag and brought forth its contents.

A large jar full of flitting shapes.

"The desert curse continues," he said, lifting the jar high above his head. With a shudder of horror, I saw what was inside.

Tarantula hawks.

Swinging his arms down in a swift arc, Zane smashed the jar on the atrium pavement before my feet. It shattered, setting the flutter of dark wings free. Before I could do more than gasp, he'd slid the glass door shut and turned the lock.

The buzz of angry wasps filled the air.

Chapter 24

I STARED, PETRIFIED, AS the insects rose and hovered, each as big as my outspread hand. Despite the desert heat filtering in from above, waves of chilling terror washed over me, numbing my brain but not my fear.

I remembered what Darren had said about the excruciating pain from a single sting being enough to drive a man insane, giving him the worst minutes of his life.

In my case, those would also be the last minutes of my life.

As the black-winged bodies darted and flapped around me, I groped in the pocket of my jeans for my EpiPen. Pulling it free, I felt a tiny rush of relief.

Until I realized it was empty.

The device that could save my life had already been discharged, the vital stimulant expelled. I looked through the glass to where Zane stood watching, one palm pressed against the transparent wall, his eyes boring into mine.

His mouth moved, forming the word, "Sorry." But his expression shone with vengeance rather than regret.

Wings brushed against my face and I dropped the useless EpiPen, crying out and moving automatically to swat at the insects. An instant too late, I realized it was exactly the wrong thing to do. The furious humming grew louder as one of the giant wasps dodged and hovered near my right ear, sending spikes of icy fear down my spine.

I thought again of old man Reavis and his crazy, frenzied display of desperate bravery. His strategy would be a death warrant for me. My best tactic would be to stand motionless, slowing even my heartbeat, if I could. I wondered if wasps could sense fear like some animals, if the smell of my terror would paint a target on my exposed flesh.

Something throbbed in my hand and I nearly screamed before remembering that I still held my cell phone. Moving slowly, in tiny increments, I tipped the screen toward my face and slanted my eyes so I could read the message appearing there.

Careful, Zane headed your way. We're coming to you now.

Slowly, cautiously, I raised the phone to the glass, sharing Madsen's message with Zane. He read it and shifted his gaze to my face. I mouthed the word, "Sorry."

Fury blazed in Zane's eyes, inflaming his features. He pounded on the glass wall of the atrium, screaming obscenities, further agitating the insects.

The droning buzz surrounding me intensified, the beating of many wings stirring the air like a threatening breeze. The fear flooding through me surged toward the breaking point as I stood frozen.

There was only one course of action left for me.

Closing my eyes, I prayed.

In those first few seconds, my panic rose and the wasps seemed to me as the demons of hell. Malevolent dark-winged angels come to inject me with venom and drag me down to their vile master.

But as I continued to fervently send my pleas heavenward, a blessed calm descended over me. Little by little, drop by drop, as morning dew, bringing a balm of relief greater than anything I had ever experienced.

I don't know how long I stood like that, with my head bowed in prayer, warmed by rays of light from above, but at some point I realized the fiendish buzzing no longer vibrated in the air around me. I heard instead a faint hiss as the atrium door slid aside.

I opened my eyes.

Zane was still there, still staring at me with vicious loathing, but his hands were cuffed behind his back and he was flanked by Madsen and his partner, Steele. I looked upward just in time to see the last of the tarantula hawks weaving and diving as they cleared the top of the glass column and flew off into the twilight sky.

Chapter 25

— · —

MORE THAN A WEEK passed before I found myself once again in the canyon, listening to the echo of horse's hooves clopping across the dry desert floor. The sun, burning down through the stone corridor, felt hot on my shoulders, its heat intensifying the scent of sagebrush and wildflowers.

In the busy days since my ordeal in the atrium, I'd seen Zane arrested and spent hours with Madsen and Steele, giving my statement and learning about the progress of their case against my best friend's killer. The little brother I'd never really known.

The crime scene team had found the trace of a boot mark on the front of Clint's shirt and matched it to Zane's Tony Lamas, suggesting that Clint's murder probably happened pretty much the way I'd imagined it.

In addition, they'd found a packet of powerful painkillers hidden away in his luggage, and traces of that same drug in the blood samples taken at the scene of Zane's stabbing.

Madsen's ballistic people had not been able to satisfactorily fire a stone arrow from the recovered crossbow, reinforcing our theory that the bow had been placed to confuse and distract from the actual method of murder. Certain tool marks, however, allowed them to connect the modifications to Zane's welding workshop.

And then, there was the splinter of stone.

Lodged in Zane's finger and matching the murder weapon exactly, it became a damning piece of evidence. On multiple levels. It was the tall tale I constructed around that splinter that drew the confession from Zane and sealed his fate.

I didn't know whether the recording I'd made of that confession would be admissible in court, but Madsen assured me they had what they needed to see justice done.

It didn't make me feel any better.

Under questioning, Mike Nichols admitted he'd been the one to tip the rock over the ledge, almost pinning me to the desert floor. He claimed it hadn't been intended to hit me, only to discourage me from completing my climb and finding him and Sarah trailing our movements.

My own scrape with death had been wholly unconnected to what happened to Clint.

Swallowing the ache that kept creeping up into my throat, I'd helped make the arrangements for Clint's funeral and memorial service, which was well-attended and well-observed. Clint had touched a lot of people and made a lot of friends. I was beyond honored that he'd considered me the best of them.

There was one more thing I felt like I should do for Clint before I left Arizona. We'd come for a reason, and Clint would want me—would expect me—to finish the search and find the Lost Dutchman. To accomplish this long sought-after feat and credit him with the discovery seemed a fitting memorial to the dynamic, adventurous man Clint had been.

So, here I was. Back in the Superstition mountains.

As on that first morning, Theta rode in front, her long hair bouncing against her back. But there was something about her stance in the saddle that spoke of sadness, a certain deflation. I felt it too. Without Clint, the expedition had lost its spark.

Still, we pushed on past midday, passing the cliff dwelling where I'd seen Clint take Theta's hand. As we rode past the entrance to the box canyon where Nichols had toppled the boulder, a shadow fell across the sun-heated stone walls of the canyon. I smelled that familiar odor, the smell of a screen door, and looked into the clouding sky.

A cold raindrop hit me in the eye. And then another and another. As the rain began pelting down, I directed Sandia toward an outcropping of rock where we might take cover.

"No," Darren shouted. "Follow me!"

Turning, he spurred his horse into a fast trot, leading us back to the cluster of cliff dwellings. Jumping off the horse, he slapped its rear and it galloped off. Theta did the same with her horse, so I followed suit with Sandia.

"The horses know how to get to the high ground and have a better chance of making it without us on their backs," Theta explained.

"What's happening?" I asked.

Darren's face was grim. "Flash flood coming," he said. "Climb."

The rain was sluicing down now, turning the dirt beneath our boots into a froth of mud. Stepping up onto the rock where I'd fallen and twisted my ankle, I pulled myself up the cliff face, hands slipping on wet stone. Grunting and heaving, I made it at last and rolled aside, clearing the way for Theta and Darren behind me.

"If you ever needed an explanation for why the natives built their houses into the cliff side," Darren said as he clambered up and over the lip of stone, "this will do it."

He started to say something else, but his words were lost in a rush of sound, a roar growing louder with each second. I stared down into the swirling maw. Where only moments before we'd stood on parched hardpan and dry sand, an angry torrent of foaming water tumbled and surged, sending great splashes of dirty spray into our sheltered spot.

The water rose at an alarming rate. If it didn't subside soon, it wouldn't take long to reach us where we crouched, watching the destructive force in fascination. I saw tree branches, old tires, and all manner of debris carried away on the violent gushing stream.

The mad course of the flood explained the formation of the canyon, the naturally carved overhangs where we'd camped or eaten lunch. And, as Darren had pointed out, the reason for the cliff dwellings.

As I watched, almost hypnotized by the swirling, thundering mass of water, I realized that whatever landmarks Jacob Waltz had indicated on his map, however helpful they might have been at the turn of the nineteenth century, they all may well have been long since obliterated.

In that moment, I accepted that the treasure, the lost gold mine of the Dutchman, would remain forever hidden. And that felt fine and fitting.

Clint and I had found the real treasure, more precious than a raft of gold. Our true friendship was the greatest prize, and he'd given me the most supreme gift one human can give another.

He'd saved my life.

And made it a life worth living.

Death could not erase his deed of devotion.

As the deafening roar of the flood diminished and the tide receded from our place of refuge, I noticed I'd been hunkering down next to the spot where, last time, I'd touched the finger marks in the bricks, made by long ago people. As before, I fitted my hand into the grooves where their fingers had been.

Reaching, connecting, and realizing that the kinship we share as humans on the planet is a very real one.

I felt Clint in that hand print. I knew he was there. That a part of him would always be with me, until we met again someday.

Until we all met again.

The sound of the rushing water died away completely as the storm ceased and the flood faded, leaving great stretches of mud and silted puddles. And now I heard them, the whisperings of the dead and departed. But they didn't frighten me. They didn't menace or threaten me.

They encouraged me. I thought I heard my grandfather's voice and my mother's aunt who'd passed away the year I turned sixteen. I grasped a small piece of comprehension at the eternal power of love, that the ties that bind us as friends and family reach beyond the dimensions of space and time.

And I knew the treasure I'd found in the mountain was mine forever—impervious to rust and moth, safe from thieving hands, and precious beyond all accounting.

I went home a rich man.

T HANK YOU FOR READING *Falling for The Lost Dutchman.*

I hope you enjoyed the story, and I invite you to visit my book page at Paraquel Press to find more suspense-packed stories. Go to https://paraquelpress.mailerpage.com/books

Also, don't forget to sign up and join the growing group of readers who've discovered the thrill of Chase! You'll get *No Rest: 14 Tales of Chilling Suspense,* as well as VIP access to updates and bonuses. Just head to joslynchase.com to get started.

Thanks again, and if you liked *Falling for The Lost Dutchman,* please consider leaving a review to help other readers find and enjoy it too.

—·—

Author's Notes

THE LEGEND OF THE LOST DUTCHMAN

This legend has all the elements that go into a fascinating mystery—lost treasure, unexplained death, and a cast of interesting characters. I enjoyed many hours digging into the background of the legend and the folklore surrounding the Superstition mountains in Arizona.

Interest in this topic was born and bred into me.

I grew up in Tucson, not all that far from the Superstition Mountains, and my father was fascinated by the legend of the Lost Dutchman's mine, regaling my siblings and me with stories about it on many occasions.

Back in those days, there was a theme park based on local myth called Legend City, just outside of Phoenix, that featured a ride inspired by the legend of the Lost Dutchman.

My family visited the park when I was a toddler and while standing in line for one of the kiddie boat rides, I managed to get loose from my parents. Somehow, I broke through the barrier and had a ball splashing around by myself in the refreshing water of the boat ride, providing some entertainment for the crowd.

It's a funny family story, but imagine my surprise when I returned to Legend City as a grade school student on a tour of some of the attractions and heard the guide tell the story of the little girl who broke through the fence to paddle in the water and amuse the guests.

I, myself, had become a legend at Legend City!

A closer look at the Dutchman

During the time I was researching this story, I wrote a blog post detailing some of my findings. If you're interested, I invite you to come on by and read the article at

https://joslynchase.com/the-enduring-legend-of-the-lost-dutchman/

I watched several episodes of a series I found on Amazon Prime, Mysteries of the Superstition Mountains. This helped Jay prepare for his role as storyteller around the campfire.

A rich source of information for me was the Tom Kollenborn Chronicles, a blog site based on the explorations of Tom Kollenborn, one of the legend's foremost experts.

http://superstitionmountaintomkollenborn.blogspot.com/2009/11/origin-of-lost-dutchmans-mine-story.html

I was also fortunate enough to watch an episode of Unsolved Mysteries on the subject of the Lost Dutchman's Mine. Sadly, it has since become unavailable.

Many books have been written on the subject, if you'd like to dig deeper, and I wish you luck!

FLASH FLOOD IN THE CANYON

My background information for the flash flood came purely through personal experience. I was twelve years old at the time, so my memory of the event is somewhat faded and colored by dramatic license, but I drew on my recollections of that day to portray the flood.

I was tubing in a canyon in New Mexico with my cousins when we heard a building roar and climbed up the cliff face to huddle on a ledge as the tidal wave of water crashed through the canyon just a few scant feet below us.

I remember watching, mesmerized by the sound and swirling, as tree branches, tires, and even an old washing machine bobbed past in the rushing flood. That experience also came in handy for me when writing scenes for *Nocturne in Ashes*, with catastrophic flooding caused by a volcanic eruption.

I hope you enjoyed **Falling for the Lost Dutchman** and I invite you to check out more of my work!

MORE BOOKS BY JOSLYN CHASE

Nocturne in Ashes

Steadman's Blind

The Tower

No Rest

What Leads A Man To Murder

For a complete listing, visit Joslyn's Book Page
at joslynchase.com

Watch the trailers on
Joslyn's YouTube channel!

SAMPLE FROM STEADMAN'S BLIND

PROLOGUE

Fifty-eight miles south of Seattle, Mt. Rainier rises to meet the clouds. Reigning queen of the landscape, she symbolizes the pristine beauty of the Pacific Northwest, robed in emerald, and crowned with diamond-sparkling snow, the graceful sweep of her slopes soaring up to draw the eye and gladden the heart.

But the benevolent appearance of the mountain masks a deadly and volatile might.

Within the reach of that power, communities nestle. Secure in the belief that life today will continue as it did yesterday, and the day before, and for so many days before that, people build houses, elect officials, establish commerce, and do all manner of things to create a haven for themselves and their loved ones.

While deep below Rainier's surface, a river of molten rock pushes up against the stratified layers, fracturing the bed of stone into splinters and sending tremors through the mountain and surrounding areas. For thousands of years, torrents of rain and melting snow have mixed with sulphuric acid, seeping into the rock, altering it into a crumbling clay-like substance, unstable and susceptible to landslides.

Fifty-six hundred years ago, Rainier's eastern flank blew sky high in the great Osceola mudslide, covering 212 square miles in a thick, acidic sludge, obliterating every living thing.

Now her western side is primed to go.

Early in the summer, the volcano woke like a fussy baby after a long nap, burping and bawling, grabbing everyone's attention, and mobilizing politicians, the media, and emergency response teams to prepare for a major catastrophe. For months, regal Rainier has entertained her surrounding human subjects like an eccentric hostess at a cocktail party. Trembling, grumbling, puffing smoke—fierce and lively one moment, silent and sulking the next.

In her shadow, life continues. People sleep through the night, get up, and go to work. Families argue, play, walk the dog, and love each other. Like the story of the boy who cried wolf, people find it easier and easier to ignore Rainier's dramatics as everyday life reclaims them. Politicians give in to pressure from loggers and business owners losing revenue due to road closures. Government agencies run out of money for maintaining watches and road blocks. Life in Seattle and surrounding communities returns to business as usual.

Only a handful of scientists and researchers remain vigilant and concerned.

They gauge the tremors beneath her, noticing how her shape is changing, like the burgeoning of a woman preparing to give birth. She is distending under the building pressure within, equalized only by the yards-thick layer of snow pack pressing down from without. They worry that the icy shell is cracking, destabilized by the earthquakes and the heat of the magma as it travels up into the throat of the volcano. They fear that a few degrees more, and the coat of snow will slide down the mountainside like butter off a hotcake, triggering an avalanche of unparalleled proportions.

They know what will happen next. The enormous weight rolling off Rainier's western shoulder will allow the inexorable pressure of gas and hot rock to spurt forth, uncontained, blowing aside the weak, altered rock in a savage eruption with a power 7500 times greater than the atomic blast at Hiroshima.

A poisonous plume of ash and gas will rise into a hideously exaggerated mushroom cloud extending miles into the sky, where the negatively charged ash will clash violently with the positively charged gas to spawn a hellish network of lightning bolts and streaking balls of fire.

It will be the deadliest day in American history—ending lives, changing lives, reminding people how precious life is.

And how precarious.

Chapter 1

Chief Deputy Randall Steadman set his jaw and ground his teeth together. Fear wrestled against frustration somewhere behind his belt buckle, stirring up a queasy tightness in his gut. For miles in front of him, traffic inched forward on streets crammed to capacity, allowing him to experience the full joys of a Portland rush hour, complete with rude hand gestures, honking horns, and blaring car stereos.

He itched to flip on the light bar and clear a path, but he wasn't behind the wheel of his service vehicle and he was out of uniform and out of his jurisdiction. He'd made the three-hour drive south after a frantic phone call from his sister.

A phone call that left him cold.

Nan was a pretty put-together gal. Whatever happened down here in Oregon had spooked her good and that scared Steadman. He'd relied on his big sister for most of his life, and now it was plain she was relying on him. For reasons that went deep—beyond standard sibling solidarity—he could not let her down.

The late summer sun beat down through the windshield of his car, canceling out the efforts of his air conditioner, and the engine temperature gauge was creeping higher than he liked to see. He switched off the AC and powered down the windows, resigned to suffering through until traffic picked up again. According to the GPS, he only had two-and-a-half miles to go before he reached the hospital.

The hospital.

Nan hadn't told him why she'd chosen that as their meeting place and she hadn't left him time to ask, but Steadman knew it couldn't be good. He dreaded what he might find when he got there. A sudden gust of diesel fumes from a truck up ahead permeated the air and Steadman felt like he might suffocate—from the smell, from the heat, from the anxious stone that pressed down inside his chest.

Whatever this was, whatever tragedy Nan faced, it surely couldn't be as bad as his gut was making it out to be.

Could it?

The red light blinked to green and Steadman let off the brake, moving forward enough to get a slight breeze across his sweaty brow. Another ten minutes and the robotic GPS voice let him know he was arriving at his destination. He pulled into the first parking spot he came across, not caring how far he had to walk. He needed that time to decompress and prepare.

Nan had texted him a room number. After checking in at the front desk, he caught the elevator up to the third floor and passed a nurse's station where a solitary head bent over a stack of medical files. The hallway was deserted. Only the smell of rubbing alcohol lingered there, following him as he made his way down the corridor to stop outside room 324.

He took a deep breath and let it trickle out, readying himself to push open that door and be strong for his sister. But before he could reach out a hand, the door swept inward and Steadman was staring at two cops in uniform. They hesitated, looking him over, and Steadman knew what they were thinking. It was all the things he would be thinking, the way you get after years on the job.

Nan pushed between them and folded Steadman in a tight embrace.

"I knew you'd get here quick," she said.

He pulled away enough to look her in the face. A reddened lump swelled beside her right temple, and the eye was shadowed by bruises, black turning purple.

"What happened?" he asked. "Were you in a car accident? Is Hank okay?"

Steadman looked beyond her to the hospital bed, swathed in sheets and shadows. The sleeping form was her husband, Hank, and Steadman got a quick impression of tubes. Lots of tubes.

Nan closed her teeth over her lips in that bulldog way she had and Steadman saw a pleading look in her eyes before her gaze dropped away. He noticed she was shivering.

"This is my brother, Chief Deputy Randall Steadman," she told the policemen. "He drove down from the Seattle area."

Steadman shook their hands, and they exchanged professional courtesies before he turned back to Nan and lifted his fingers to her damaged cheek.

"What happened?" he repeated.

There was a pause before she answered. "It wasn't a car accident," she said. "We were attacked."

"Attacked? What—"

"I'm sorry, Rand." She staggered under his grip and raised a shaky hand to her throat. "I really need some coffee and something to eat." She turned to the officers. "If there's nothing else you need from me, I think I'll go to the cafeteria."

"Of course, Mrs. Meninger. We'll be in touch."

They nodded their goodbyes and left. Nan clutched Steadman's arm as she watched the policemen stride down the corridor. He felt her tremble like a sapling in a windstorm, but she didn't speak until the men stopped at the elevator and punched the call button.

"I'll go get my purse," she whispered. "We need to talk."

Chapter 2

Nan's cup of coffee sat untouched on the table in front of her, the rising tendrils of vapor waning as it grew cold. Steadman watched her face, the leaden lump in his stomach growing with each moment that passed. She was tough, his sister, and the bones of her skull stood out under pallid skin like a Mt. Rushmore monument, solid and unmoving. But there was fear in her eyes, tinged with despair. That alarmed him, and the swelling at her temple and blackened eye sent anger swirling through his growing sense of dread.

"Tell me what happened, Nan," he prompted. "When, where, and—if possible—who."

A wash of color came into her face, and he was relieved to see there was still some spirit left in her.

"Oh, I know who well enough," she said, her voice shot through with acid. "They made no effort to disguise themselves."

"Did you tell the police?"

She pressed her lips together, blanching them white. Her nostrils flared as she drew a breath through her nose. "I did not."

The heavy lump in his gut sank. "What's going on, Nan? I guess you've got a lot to tell me, but first I want to know about Hank. How bad is it?"

She closed her eyes, face twisting as she wrestled her emotions. Steadman covered her shaking hand with his own and waited. Almost a minute passed before she swallowed hard and opened her mouth to speak.

"They kicked him. Two bastards taking turns with their heavy boots." Her voice went squeaky, and she paused, taking a deep breath. "He's got four cracked ribs, a broken arm, a broken nose, and a ruptured spleen. He lost three teeth and his face is unrecognizable. He'll never again be the pretty boy I married."

Steadman squeezed her hand. Bad as it was, he had feared worse. "Well, Nan," he said, hoping to lighten the mood, "that ship sailed a long time ago."

She gave him a weak smile. "Don't I know it. But—" A little sob escaped her lips and she bit down hard, staunching the flow. "I love him so much, Rand."

"I know, Sis. I know."

A loud clatter reverberated through the room as an attendant deposited a load of clean trays into a rack at the head of the cafeteria line. Steadman watched an elderly couple pry one from the top of the stack and begin working their shaky way along the path of options, consulting each other with every choice. Hank and Nan would grow old together like that—sweet to each other, caring, united.

He turned his gaze back to Nan. "Hank will be okay, then. His prognosis is good, right?"

Her lips thinned to a grim line and again he saw that spark of color come into her face.

"He'll survive. Until they come for him again."

"Why would they do that, Nan? Who are these guys?"

"They're sharks."

"You mean, like loan sharks."

She nodded. "Yes, and worse. I'm not sure what all they're into, but they're bad news."

"How on earth did Hank get mixed up with them?"

She sighed. "You know Ronnie's in his second year at MIT."

Steadman stared at her. "Hank borrowed college funds from a loan shark?"

She leveled that big sister glare at him across the table. "He's not stupid, Rand. It didn't happen like you think. Hank got sucked in, little by little, by pros who know just where to put the pressure."

Despite the anxiety that gnawed at his gut, Steadman admired Nan for standing by her man. They might be going down, but they were going down together. He hoped he could find a way to throw them a lifeline.

"Start at the beginning, Nan," he said, trying to keep his voice free from any trace of judgment, "and put me in the picture."

She canted her lower lip and blew out a frustrated sigh that reached her bangs, fluttering them as it passed. "As you know, Hank's a night manager at the Hilton. In the course of his business, he became aware that these guys were running an illegal high-stakes poker game from their hotel suite. Their leader is a man they call Honest Abe, and no one even tries to keep a straight face about it. He offered Hank a thousand dollars to look the other way."

She broke off, swirls of red staining her cheeks. "It sounds terrible, the way I put it," a pleading note crept into her voice, "but you've got to understand there was a lot going on for us. We were squeezed pretty tight with no room to breathe or see our way clear. Car broke down, late on the mortgage, bills coming due, and time to pay another round of tuition. College costs more than a house, these days. Hank thought it would be a onetime deal. He let it slide."

Steadman saw all too clearly where this was going. It was like letting the camel put one foot inside the tent. Pretty soon you've got the whole animal on your lap and you're drowning in sand.

"I can see the wheels churning inside your head, Rand, and whatever you're thinking, it's probably not far off the mark. The games continued, the payouts got bigger, and by the time Hank realized how deep he was in, he couldn't get out. He was complicit. So when they stopped paying him there was nothing he could do about it. They had him by the balls."

Steadman grimaced. "Ouch. So why'd they beat him up? Did he end up ratting them out?"

Nan clenched her fists on the table in front of her, nearly spilling the cup of congealing coffee.

"I only wish he had. No, we'd come to count on that extra money, and when they stopped paying for Hank's silence, it hurt. But Abe wasn't finished with Hank. He brought him into his fancy suite, buttered him up, told him the hush money had stopped because he was one of them now, part of the team, and he was welcome at the table. They'd even stake him the first game."

Steadman groaned. "You've got to be kidding. What the hell was he thinking, Nan?"

She scowled at him, her teeth going up over her lip in that classic Nan expression of stubborn annoyance.

"You don't know these guys. They're urbane and charismatic. Car salesman types that can convince you they're your best pal while they're sizing you up for a coffin. Hank figured it wouldn't hurt to play that first game, with their money. He cleaned up, too. Brought home a pile, that night."

Steadman snorted. "Naturally, Nan. That's how it's done. He was hooked, right?"

She sighed. "By the nose. They sucked him dry, and then some." She rubbed at a spot on her forehead with two shaking fingers. "We're putting the house on the market and hoping it sells before they come back to break Hank's legs."

"Oh heavens, Nan," Steadman felt a vein of cold misery spreading through him. "Why didn't you tell the police?"

She gave him a pointed look. "That's the first thing they warned us about. Told us they had police protection, key officers on the payroll, and it would only go harder on us if we squealed."

Steadman swallowed and tossed through his mental inventory for some way to bring her comfort.

"They're not going to hurt you so bad you can't cough up the money. They want you operational, Nan. It sounds like they're giving you some sort of deadline?"

"Six weeks. They said if we didn't pay up in six weeks, Hank's a dead man."

He patted her hand. "They're not going to kill him, Sis. That's just to scare you."

Her face crumpled, and she bit her lip, silent tears spilling from her reddened eyes. She brushed them off and stared across the table at Steadman, her jaw hardening.

"Jeb Openshaw, the man Hank replaced at the hotel—he died in a hit-and-run accident. A newspaper clipping about the incident was left in an envelope on Hank's desk. If they don't get their money, they cut their losses and make an example."

Steadman saw the shudder that ran through her. He moved his chair next to hers and wrapped his arms around her, rocking her, wondering what the hell his next move should be. After a few moments, she pulled away and smoothed the hair back from her face, sitting taller in her chair, chin lifted.

"I spent a lot of time thinking," she said. "While Hank was in surgery, while I waited beside his broken body for you to arrive." She speared Steadman with her big sister gaze.

"And I came up with a plan."

Chapter 3

Newly christened Detective Cory Frost tried balancing his breakfast in one hand while pulling open the door to the training room with the other. The two slabs of peanut butter toast were no problem, held firmly together, face to face, and wrapped in a paper towel. And the pint of chocolate milk rested firmly against his wrist. It was the orange that defeated him.

He lost his grip on the soft-ball-sized fruit and it bounced, then rolled into the path of a sergeant in a hurry who kicked it back in Frost's direction.

"Sorry about that," Frost mumbled, bending down to retrieve the orange.

The notebook tucked beneath his elbow slid down the side of his uniform trousers and splayed open on the floor. He sighed. Picking it up, he used it as a tray and arranged the breakfast items on top, except for the orange, which he tried to cram into the pocket of his jacket. Again, it escaped him, but he managed to scoop it from the air before it hit the floor, bringing him into a crouching position like a catcher at home plate.

Before he could rise, a shapely pair of ankles appeared in front of his face.

"That's some impressive juggling, Detective. Do you do birthday parties?"

He stood, feeling his face go hot. The uniformed woman regarding him with an expression half scorn, half amusement, was a heart-stopper. Glowing, cocoa complexion, glossy dark hair cascading in a smooth sweep over a perfect brow, lips a cover girl would kill for. Frost stared.

The woman raised an eyebrow. "I'll hold the door for you," she said, reaching for the handle, "but I get half the orange."

Frost froze like a deer in the headlights. Not a single clever response came to him, but he was saved from saying something stupid when the door burst open, nearly knocking them down, and Sheriff Polander glared at the both of them.

"Hurry it up, people. We're about to start."

Frost waggled his eyebrows, getting a grin in return. He held tight to his breakfast and stepped into the room after the woman, getting another glimpse of her stunning figure. His heart sank when he saw the crowded tables with no two seats together. He'd started to imagine sharing his day—as well as his orange—with his captivating colleague, but they were forced apart, to opposite sides of the room. He took a seat at the front table to the left of the podium and laid out his items, noticing that the woman was across the aisle and well behind him.

He hadn't seen her before, but he was brand new in the detective division and still had a lot of people to meet. In the brief moment he'd been with her, he noticed she wore no ring on her left hand and the name on her tag was longish and started with a J. And she was gorgeous and witty and...

He crushed a mental boot down on these thoughts. He needed to reclaim his focus, get his head in the right place or he'd end up back in Patrol for another rotation. He'd worked hard for this promotion and it jazzed him to be part of Investigations. He opened his notebook and wrote the date at the top of the page, ready to record the salient points of the training.

"Jamieson!"

The sheriff bellowed the name to the back rows. "Did Chief Deputy Steadman come over with you?"

"No, sir." Frost recognized her voice and turned in his seat. Jamieson.

"He's on emergency leave," she continued. "Had a family issue down in Portland."

"Why am I just hearing about this now? He's supposed to give the potential hazard report."

"Yes sir, I know. He asked me to apologize, and he prepped me to do it."

"Is that right?" The sheriff took a sip of coffee. "I want you here up front, then. Dooley," he gestured to Frost's table mate. "Trade places with Jamieson, if you would."

"Sure thing, Sheriff."

And just like that, Frost was sitting next to the most beautiful girl in the room, trying to listen and stay focused on the subject at hand. His peanut butter toast went untouched, cold and forgotten.

But he peeled the orange, keeping the skin intact, and laid a perfect half on top, sliding it in her direction like a supplicant's offering to his goddess.

Chapter 4

Steadman choked on a mouthful of lukewarm coffee, getting half of it down, spewing half of it back into the cup. He coughed, working to clear his throat so he could spit some words out, though he had no idea what he might say. The suggestion his sister had just made was the most ridiculous thing he'd ever heard.

"There's no need to be so dramatic about it, Rand," she chided, handing him a napkin. "It's a pragmatic plan that has a good chance of working."

"In what universe?" Steadman asked, his head reeling. "I don't play poker, Nan."

"Yes, but how hard can it be?" she countered. "For you, I mean. You're trained to observe and interpret body language. You know when people are lying, all the little things they do to give themselves away. Nobody can bluff you."

He stared at her. "Nan, this isn't television. Poker is a whole different thing and—listen carefully because here's the important part—I don't play it. I barely know a full house from a straight flush."

"But you can learn. You live right around the corner from that big casino. You can do some research on the internet and practice the skills at your friendly neighborhood poker tables."

"For Pete's sake, woman—have you gone insane?"

Steadman felt a pressure building inside his chest. He took a deep breath and let it roll out of him, rubbing the muscles at the back of his neck in an effort to relax.

"Nan, I understand you're upset and worried, and you have every right to be. You're looking for solutions to what feels like an insurmountable problem. I get that. But this plan sounds like a recipe for even more trouble. I can't believe—"

"Rand, just shut up for a minute. I told myself all these same things while I sat in a cold, hard hospital chair waiting for my husband to come out of surgery after being beaten within an inch of his life. These are very bad men, playing a whole lot of angles, and the only way to escape this is to beat them at their own game—and that's poker."

Steadman sighed and dropped his head to rest in the palm of his hand. How did she still have this ability to reduce him to younger brother status, reminding him she was in charge?

"It takes money, Nan, to win at poker," he pointed out. "And we don't have any."

She was nodding. "I know. I had mom's jewelry appraised when this whole mess started. I hoped I wouldn't have to sell, but I can get close to six thousand dollars for it. You can take that to the local casino and parlay it into a bigger stake. Hank said the buy-in at Bernie's table is ten thousand."

She really had been thinking about this, scrambling to cover all the bases.

"This'll be second nature to you, Rand," she continued. "I know it will. I heard you telling Hank about that non-verbal communication seminar you attended in San Diego. Four days, Rand. Four days of intensive training so you can read the unintentional signals people give off. If anyone can do this, it's you, little brother." She dropped her hand over his and squeezed. "And you're the only one who cares about me enough to even try."

And there it was, Nan going for the heart string, twanging away on familial duty, love, and the ever-powerful chord of guilt. They both knew she still held an ace up her sleeve, a card she could play with perfect assurance he'd comply. A card with Thad's name on it.

He wouldn't make her do that. Reaching that deep into a painful memory would leave a gash in both of them that might never heal. He dug the palms of his hands into his eyes and rubbed, hardly believing the sentence that was forming on his lips.

"You sell mom's jewels, Nan, and I'll see what I can do about learning some poker."

As he spoke the words, he made a promise to himself as well. He'd do some digging behind the scenes. There had to be another way around this problem.

If you enjoyed this sample, you'll love where *Steadman* goes from here. Grab the book and enjoy the ride!

About the Author

Joslyn Chase is a prize-winning author of mysteries and thrillers. Any day where she can send readers to the edge of their seats, chewing their fingernails to the nub and prickling with suspense, is a good day in her book.

Joslyn's story, "Cold Hands, Warm Heart," was chosen by Amor Towles as one of the *Best Mystery Stories of the Year 2023*. Her short stories have appeared in *Alfred Hitchcock's Mystery Magazine, Fiction River Magazine, Mystery, Crime, and Mayhem, Mystery Magazine,* and *Pulphouse Fiction,* among others.

Known for her fast-paced suspense fiction, Joslyn's books are full of surprising twists and delectable turns. You will find her riveting novels most anywhere books are sold.

Her love for travel has led Joslyn to ride camels through the Nubian desert, fend off monkeys on the Rock of Gibraltar, and hike the Bavarian Alps. But she still believes that sometimes the best adventures come in getting the words on the page and in the thrill of reading a great story.

Join the growing group of readers who've discovered the thrill of Chase! Sign up for Joslyn's readers' group and get VIP access to great bonuses—like your free copy of *No Rest: 14 Tales of Chilling Suspense*—as well as updates and first crack at new releases.

Go to joslynchase.com to get started.

Falling for The Lost Dutchman

Published by Paraquel Press

https://paraquelpress.mailerpage.com/

ISBN: 978-1-952647-17-8

Cover photo by Jaime Reimer, pexels.com

Cover design by Caryl Giles

Thank you.